ANGEL
AND
THE NUN

An enthralling crime mystery full of twists

ROGER SILVERWOOD

Yorkshire Murder Mysteries Book 29

Joffe Books, London
www.joffebooks.com

First published in Great Britain in 2022

© Roger Silverwood 2022

ISBN: 978-1-80405-629-5

ONE

The Convent of the Holy Reliquary of the Finger of Saint Ethel
Bromersley, South Yorkshire
Monday, 14 November, 2 a.m.

The freezing night fog was cold and unpleasant. It was as cold and unpleasant as the murderer who stalked the dark corridors of the convent.

Sister Teresa opened her eyes, not knowing what had awakened her. She blinked. Very little was visible in the darkness of her room. She rolled over and peered in the direction of the alarm clock on her bedside locker. She could just make out the luminous clock hands and was satisfied she had another three hours before rising. She rolled back on to her other side, pulled up the duvet, snuggled down and closed her eyes.

Moments later she heard a piercing scream. She held her breath and listened. Her heart beat in her ears like a drum.

Her hand went to the silver crucifix on the chain round her neck. She gripped it tightly and murmured a silent prayer.

The scream, she thought, must have been from one of the other nuns.

1

Teresa's breathing was fast and irregular. She listened, anxious not to mask any further sound. What should she do? If one of her fellow nuns was in trouble . . .

She switched on the bedside light and swung her legs out of bed. It was colder than she had expected. She shivered as she put her warm feet into her cold sandals. She reached out for her dark blue dressing gown and put it on.

She went out of her room, switched on the landing lights, then floated swiftly down the long corridor, her pulse racing, passing several doors to the other bedrooms until she reached the room at the end.

She tapped on the door. 'Reverend Mother?' she said. 'Reverend Mother?'

Teresa turned the knob and the door opened, which surprised her. It was usually bolted at night.

'Reverend Mother, sorry to disturb you.' She reached up to the light switch on the wall. 'But—'

She stopped. Reverend Mother wasn't there. But the blankets on the bed were turned down and there was a depression in the pillow.

Teresa put her hand on the bedclothes. They were still warm.

A voice from behind startled her. It almost sounded like a reprimand.

'Whatever are you doing, Sister?'

Teresa gasped. But it was only Sister Precious — an old and very small nun who had been Reverend Mother at Saint Ethel's Convent for many years; she had stepped back from the post when she reached her eighty-sixth year. She was an absolute authority on everything to do with Church matters, the Bible and the reliquary.

'Feeling the temperature of the bed. What did you think I was doing?' Teresa replied sharply. 'I'm looking for the Reverend Mother!'

Precious said, 'She might be in the chapel . . . she goes there sometimes if she can't sleep.'

Teresa nodded. They both made their way along the landing and down the stairs to the front door, which was unlocked. They went outside.

The sky was clear and the moon shone brightly.

Teresa walked quickly across the twinkling frost-covered pathway towards the small chapel. Precious, balking at the slippery condition of the path, stopped and impatiently called, 'Wait for me.'

Teresa wrinkled her nose and dutifully ran back. She put her arm under Precious's and half supported, half dragged the little old nun along the slippery path.

They could see that the chapel door was ajar. A small light shone out on to the path. Precious pulled away from Teresa, pushed in front of her and ran into the chapel.

The only light was from two altar candles.

They were relieved to see the Reverend Mother at the altar rail. The two nuns genuflected in the presence of the holy cross and approached her.

She was on her knees before the cross, in her nightdress and dressing gown.

The Reverend Mother was a pretty woman in her forties, popular with her wards; despite her relative youth, she had been their superior for three years and was thought to be one of the best leaders the convent had ever had.

Precious and Teresa walked up the short aisle with the intention of joining her at the rail, but stopped abruptly at what they saw: a priest lying very still on his back on the floor across the front of the altar. He had blood on his collar and face.

They gasped and looked at each other.

'Father Richard.' Precious's eyes shone, reflecting the mean light of the candles.

Teresa nodded.

Then the Reverend Mother rose to her feet from the altar rail. She turned to face them, pointed at the door and put her finger to her lips, to indicate that they should leave the chapel in silence. Then she quickly leaned over the altar rail again, looking round the little chapel, and at the body of the priest.

The two shocked nuns turned towards the door and went out into the night as the Reverend Mother blew out the candles behind them. They waited and shivered as she locked the door and put the big key in her dressing-gown pocket.

'What's happened, Reverend Mother?' Teresa said. 'Are you all right?'

Precious put her hands up to her face. 'Oh, my dear Julia.' The older nun often forgot to address the Reverend Mother by her correct title — the force of habit was perhaps too strong.

'Let's go into the kitchen,' the Reverend Mother said. 'I'm frozen . . . I expect you are too. We must check on the others . . . make sure they're all safe.'

'And we must check on the reliquary,' added Precious. 'Ensure that the casket has not been interfered with.'

* * *

It was 8.35 a.m. when Detective Inspector Michael Angel ended his call from the super and set the phone back on its cradle. He put on his hat and coat and went out into the corridor to the open-plan office, looking around for Detective Sergeant Carter. He caught her eye, and she came over to him.

'Put your coat on, Flora. We've got a dead body to look at. Meet me at the front.'

'Right, sir.'

Three minutes later they were on their way.

'This is an unusual one for us, Flora,' Angel said as he reached top gear in the BMW. 'A dead man, a priest, has been found in the chapel at Saint Ethel's Convent — the Reverend Mother found his body.'

'Is that the place with the big stone walls all round it and big brown wooden gates that are always closed?'

He nodded, then blinked several times. 'It's a big building for such a small community — only five nuns, so I'm told. Do you know, I've lived in Bromersley all my life, passed that place hundreds of times, but I've never ever seen those gates open.'

'Me neither,' Carter said. 'And it's got a big, strange name.'

'Yes. The Convent of the Holy Reliquary of the Finger of Saint Ethel.'

'Well, what does it mean?'

'Reliquary means safe place — or special place for a relic — and the relic is . . . in this case, a finger of Saint Ethel. But don't ask me any more.'

'Is the finger valuable, then, sir?'

Angel thought for a moment. 'Well, yes and no. I can understand that to some people it might be thought to add weight to their prayers to have relics of holy people near them when they pray, or to have them close by to protect them from something they may fear, but . . .' He stopped there, thoughtfully.

'But not much of a market value, for the less devout?'

'I really don't know.' He added quickly, 'Brace yourself, Flora. We're here.'

He slowed the car down and turned the wheel. 'Pick up your clipboard.'

Carter said, 'And surprise, surprise, the gates are open!'

They were received at the door by an attractive young nun, very tall, who introduced herself as Sister Emma. She promptly showed them into the Reverend Mother's little office.

Introductions over, Angel said, 'We had better see the victim first, if you don't mind.'

The Reverend Mother picked up a large key and led the two police officers out of the back door of the main convent building, down the short walk to the chapel next door.

'Didn't you think to call a doctor, Reverend Mother?' Angel asked as she put the key in the chapel door lock.

'I have had eight years as a nurse, Inspector,' she said. 'I know a dead body when I see one. There was no pulse and he wasn't breathing.'

Angel nodded.

Carter was making notes on a clipboard.

'And you said that you knew who it was?'

'Father Morgan. He was our priest. Only appointed last month. These days, a priest has such a large parish. Father Morgan had eight churches and this small convent to oversee. It's too much for one person. So he had only just got round to visiting us.'

She pushed open the chapel door and went inside.

Angel and Carter followed her in. The sergeant thought it was colder inside the chapel than it was outside.

The Reverend Mother pointed towards the front of the chapel. 'He's on the floor in front of the altar rail on the right. You'll see.'

Angel went up the aisle and inspected the dead man. He briefly touched the priest's neck. It was cold. He then returned to the back of the chapel. With a nod of his head, he invited Carter to view the scene.

She did so briefly, then returned, looked at the nun and said, 'Where has the blood come from?'

'I think he has a wound in his chest. I didn't look closely.' Then she said, 'If you've both seen all you need to see here, perhaps we could retire to my study, which is much warmer . . . and I'll organise some coffee.'

Angel smiled and said, 'That would be very nice, Mother.'

They came out of the chapel and crossed to the main building, when Sister Precious came shuffling down the corridor.

'Excuse me,' she said. 'But there's more police at the door. A Detective Sergeant Taylor says he has to—'

'Thank you, Sister. That'll be the SOCO — the scene-of-crime officer,' Angel said. 'He'll need to be here with others to examine the scene and the victim.'

The Reverend Mother said, 'Very well. Sister Precious, let them in and direct them to the chapel. It is open.'

Precious stiffened, tried to make herself bigger than she was. 'Should we be letting all and sundry walk over all that we hold as private and . . . and sacred? Have you told Bishop Letterman about all this?'

The Reverend Mother's face tightened. 'He is away at present. I have left a message. And, Sister Precious, these intrusions have to be allowed. These examinations *have* to be done. Let them in and direct them to the chapel. Stay with them, if you think it necessary.'

Precious shook her head, sniffed and shuffled away, muttering.

Angel said, 'Reverend Mother, excuse me asking, but which Bishop's purview does your convent fall under?'

'Bishop John Letterman — we take our spiritual direction and teaching from him and he also overlooks our general welfare.'

'I see. I must see him very soon.' He looked at Sergeant Carter, who was writing away as they spoke. 'How well did you know Father Morgan?'

'He only made his presence known yesterday, Inspector. He phoned me and told me he would like to see all the sisters. There are only five of us. I said that that is easily arranged and that we would very much like him to celebrate the Eucharist in our chapel as soon as convenient. Which he did, at Vespers — that's five o'clock. It was very moving. I have been distributing the holy communion while there has been no priest available, with the permission of the Bishop, but I am but a poor substitute for an ordained representative of God. Then he joined us for tea, and after that he left.'

'Where did he go?'

'He was staying at Mrs Jago's bed and breakfast temporarily. That's in Tunistone. She has a spare bedroom. And she likes spoiling clergy, particularly male clergy, but she's very respectable. Done it for years.'

'I will also need to interview the other nuns.'

'Yes, of course, Inspector. Our sitting room would be the only room suitable.'

* * *

Angel phoned Bishop Letterman, who was distressed at the news but unable to say anything that would help Angel to discover the priest's murderer. The Bishop said that the Reverend Richard Morgan was a good priest, a good man from a good family. He was unmarried. He offered to inform his parents.

The interviews were not very useful either. The nuns didn't know the dead priest.

Angel finished interviewing the last nun at 5 p.m., and then left Carter to liaise with SOCO while he drove home in a thoroughly bad temper.

None of them knew anything, saw anything or did anything until they heard the scream. The convent doors, the main entrance doors and the side gate were locked at about 8 o'clock after Compline. It would have been perfectly possible to scale the six foot wall with a rope or a ladder, but both the convent and the chapel were locked according to the Reverend Mother. And there were no signs of forced entry. So it looked to Angel that the murder had to be an inside job. One of the five sisters. Finding a motive and evidence was going to be difficult. He wasn't pleased.

He drove the car into his garage, pulled down the door and locked it.

He opened the back door of the bungalow and went in.

There was an inviting smell of hot food cooking. He followed it into the kitchen.

Mary, his wife, appeared behind him.

She had dark brown hair and a pretty face. 'Got the sack?' she said teasingly.

Angel looked at her and frowned.

She said, 'You're home early . . . well, early for you.'

Angel smiled. 'To see you, my darling.' He gave her a quick kiss on the lips and a squeeze, then crossed to the cupboard and took out a tumbler.

Mary smiled briefly, then her face took on a serious expression. 'I've had a phone call.'

He noted her face, turned back to the fridge and said, 'Who was it from? Her Majesty's Revenue and Customs?'

She didn't appreciate the joke. 'No. Of course not.'

He half closed his eyes and pursed his lips. 'Your mother? No. It couldn't have been your mother, she's passed on.'

Mary almost laughed but managed to hold it back. 'No!' she snapped.

He opened the fridge door, took out a bottle of German beer and said, 'The electricity board. Price going up again?'

Her jaw stiffened. Her eyes grew wide and she stared at him.

Angel said, 'Are you going to tell me . . . or do I have to go on?'

He held the bottle of beer against the opener fixed to the wall by the sink, raised it, then lowered it, and the top was off. He then poured some beer into the glass.

Mary came up close to him. 'My sister.'

As soon as he heard those two words, his face creased up. He tried not to look as if he was standing over an open sewer.

Angel grunted. 'Miriam. What does she want now?'

'That's not very nice of you to say a thing like that . . . implying that she's always on the cadge.'

'Well she *is*!'

Mary hesitated then said, 'You don't have to *say* so in . . . that . . . that way.'

'What other way is there to put it?'

'Tell the truth, now. You don't like Miriam. You never have.'

'Actually I do. Sometimes. But she's like that girl with a curl.'

Mary frowned. 'What girl with a curl?'

'It's an old nursery rhyme. There was a little girl who had a little curl right in the middle of her forehead. When she was good—'

'Miriam has never had a curl in the middle of her forehead.'

Angel squeezed his eyebrows in surprise.

Then he said, 'Your sister lives her life like a butterfly. Flitting here and flitting there. Not sure where to land. Always in trouble. She always needs something. If it isn't a man, it's money. She had a marvellous job as the PA to that man, Piggy Thomson or Benny Fromson or whatever his name was, chairman to that big Scottish finance company . . . Top Hat pension, company car, expense allowance as long as your arm. But as soon as *he* got married, she left. Since then she's been in and out of work doing anything she fancied. And she's had more men than . . . well . . . I don't know how those two kids of hers have survived it all.'

'You don't understand her. That's your trouble.'

He shook his head, took a long drink of the beer then said, 'Well, what was the phone call about? And I bet she asked you to call her because she'd run out of credit.'

Mary ignored the last question. 'She wants us to go up next Wednesday, stay in her house and look after . . . well, supervise Kate and Will, look after the dog and keep the house safe for a few days.'

Angel frowned. 'Why? Where's she going?'

'She desperately wants to go on a three-day painting course. It's held in hotels near beauty spots in the north of Scotland. It's conducted by a leading painter. Now, you know how she loves her painting. She has a gift. She has sold a few landscapes, you know. She wants to paint full-time. Come on, Michael, I know how much you like Edinburgh. We can go off for trips in the daytime. You can take Monty to the beach for his exercise.'

Angel wrinkled his nose. 'Look, Mary . . . it all sounds very tempting, and I would no doubt be able to get time off, if it was an emergency. But there's been a recent development in the town . . . the murder of a priest.'

TWO

The next day, Tuesday, 15 November, there was a knock on Angel's office door.

It was his good friend and long-time adviser Dr Mac, a short, white-haired Scot who was the pathologist for the Bromersley area. He was always pleased to see him.

'Sit down, Mac. Have you finished the post mortem?'

He nodded and sat down. 'Aye, it's all in here.' He waved a thin, light-brown paper file at him. 'Richard Morgan, aged forty years. Stabbed with a stiletto knife. Easy to slip into the flesh and easy to withdraw.'

Angel blinked. 'A stiletto? Unusual, these days. Was the weapon still in the victim?'

'No. But you can tell by the size of the wound. In addition, the murderer might have some medical knowledge or was simply lucky. The point of the stiletto entered the pericardium and the left ventricle of the heart, so the victim died immediately.'

'SOCO tell me that the fingerprint evidence suggests he spent some time holding on to the altar rail, possibly kneeling there to pray. Does that help us understand the position he was in when he was attacked?'

'Well . . .' the pathologist said thoughtfully. 'The stab wound was in his front. So the killer might have approached from the altar, but it would be awkward to attack over the railing.'

Angel rubbed his chin. 'How tall was the priest, Mac?'

The pathologist consulted the file. 'Six foot four,' he said.

'A big chap, eh? The murderer would also have to be tall to deliver such a blow if they were both in a standing position. Would it be feasible to suggest that the attack came from behind? I mean, suppose the priest was kneeling at the altar and the murderer approached from behind and above, so to speak; could he have leaned over the victim's shoulder and stabbed him?'

Mac nodded. 'I think that's very likely, Michael. Of course, I can't say that it did happen that way.'

'So there is no certain indication as to the height of the assailant?'

'None,' Mac said.

'According to Sister Teresa, she heard the Reverend Mother's scream — the moment at which she found the body — at two o'clock on the morning of the fourteenth. Mother said he was stone cold. Do you have a time of death yet?'

'It was five degrees in that chapel. I have taken that into the calculation of the figures and I estimate that he was murdered on the evening of the thirteenth between ten o'clock and midnight.'

'Was there anything else of interest?'

The doctor screwed up his face thoughtfully. 'No. I don't think so.'

Angel turned the corners of his mouth down. 'That means I haven't a single line of enquiry to work on. All I've got are five nuns as suspects, and none of them has a motive or an alibi. They are all over five foot six tall — except one, Sister Precious, who is hardly strong enough to blow out a candle.'

'It wouldn't take much strength to push a stiletto into soft flesh. It would have been a matter of knowledge — *where* to push it in.'

Angel was still downcast.

'Sounds tough, Michael, but you've been here before,' the doctor reassured him. 'And there is one hope.'

'What's that?'

'The lab *might* be able to get the DNA of the murderer from the samples taken from the priest's body and clothes. We'll just have to wait and see.'

* * *

Meanwhile, on the other side of Bromersley, two big men in overcoats pushed their way past hanging racks of books in the doorway to the little magazine and paperback shop that was squashed between the Northern Bank and Bromersley Building Society.

A little man in the shop wearing a scruffy raincoat and in need of a bath had been passing the time fingering through some of the glossy new photographic titles. He looked up at the two men. When he recognised them, his muscles tightened, his mouth dropped open and his eyes bulged out of their sockets. He scurried out of the shop like a frightened rat.

The older of the two men was big. He wore a black overcoat and a Homburg. He had a permanent smirk which made him seem to be always smiling. However, he rarely smiled. His eyes were frequently shiny, rarely blinking; to anyone in his sights, they appeared all-seeing, and they seemed to emit light when he said something he wanted to emphasise.

He approached the counter.

The younger man closed the shop door, bolted it and took an interest in the full wall display of magazines nearest to him.

A skinny man in a brown overcoat came from the back room to a position behind the counter.

'Can I help you?' he said.

The older man said, 'Are you the proprietor?'

The thin man stuck out his chest. 'Yes. Melvyn Minter.'

'My name is Brown, Melvyn. Behind me taking an interest in your stock is my assistant, Mr Smith. I'm from the Best Insurance Company . . .'

Melvyn Minter sniffed and said, 'Ah, well, I have enough insurance, thank you.'

'Ah, but this is highly specialised insurance, Mel. It is fully comprehensive. And it is only a hundred pounds a week.'

Minter's eyes showed that he had finally sensed trouble. His heart beat a little faster. 'As I have already told you, I have enough insurance,' he said.

'Well, Mel, I would like you to think about it for a minute. Just supposing a car was driven at speed into the front of your shop? Are you covered for that?'

Minter sensed that that was a threat. He felt a hot, heavy brick in his chest and it was throbbing.

'Think about it, Mel,' Brown said. 'It would shut you down. All right, supposing some of your magazines were damaged in a spontaneous fire?'

At that moment, Brown stood back to reveal flames and smoke among the display of magazines and books near the shop doorway where Smith had been standing.

'It could start just like that, Mel.'

Minter's eyebrows shot up. The back of his hand went to his open mouth.

'Oh my goodness!' he said. His jaw clenched and his face muscles tightened. He looked from one man to the other.

Each man stood there, motionless, with deadpan faces.

Minter rushed into the back of the shop and appeared seconds later with a bowl of water. He raced down the length of the counter, rounded the end and passed in front of Smith, who put out his foot.

Minter tripped over it, stumbled and fell, the water spilling on himself and across the shop floor. His spectacles slipped off and landed on the wet lino-covered floor.

Brown looked on.

Smith grinned. 'Oh dear me. That was clumsy, Mel.'

Minter fumbled around for his spectacles, found them, picked himself up, and grabbed the empty bowl and rushed out back for more water.

At this point, Brown, who had been scanning the walls of the shop, spotted a security camera high up on the wall behind the counter. Minter emerged from the back carrying another bowl of water.

'We'll be back, Mel,' Brown called. 'And I should have a look at your cover for broken windows.'

Smith took a hammer out of his pocket and smashed one of the panes in the shop door as he passed it. Shards of glass clattered on to the step.

'Only a hundred pounds a week, Mel,' Brown said, 'and you'd be covered for fire, broken windows and everything else. And I shouldn't go to the police, Mel, or your accidental damage could get *really* dangerous.'

The two men turned and went out of the shop.

Melvyn Minter went across to the door, closed it, bolted it, went up to the places on the wall where the magazines were still burning and smoking and dowsed them thoroughly, then ran back for a refill of water. For twenty minutes or so he moved around dousing the area until he was satisfied the fire was extinguished and that the shop was absolutely safe.

He had to open the shop door to get rid of the smoke.

Several customers came in, noticed the mess and the smell and asked Melvyn Minter the cause. He played it down as much as he could and set about tidying up the display and removing all unsalable stock between making the occasional sale.

When the last customer left at five thirty, Melvyn locked the door, and looked round at the wet and dirty floor, the area of wall that had been set on fire and the black plastic bin almost full of magazines damaged by fire or water, with a value of several hundred pounds. He slumped down on a stool behind the counter, shook his head, removed his spectacles and wiped his wet eyes on the back of his hand. The relative quietness and momentary inaction allowed him time to notice the throbbing hot lump in his chest.

* * *

The following morning, Wednesday, 16 November, the Reverend Mother was busy at her desk opening the convent's post when the door opened and the diminutive figure of Sister Precious came in.

She started talking before she had closed the door.

'Julia,' she began, 'I really must ask you how I can prepare a meal without food. The good Lord has always provided, but on this occasion the ingredients for our main meal today have not yet arrived.'

The Reverend Mother threw down her pen, stood up, closed her eyes briefly, clasped her hands in front of her at her chest and said, 'Sister Precious, I have many times asked you to knock and wait for a response from me to admit you when it is convenient. It is not only a courtesy — probably the only courtesy I get in this community — I might have been at my own devotions, I could have had a guest here, I could have had—'

'Julia,' Precious interrupted, 'this is a matter of great, can I say very great, importance. We work hard and need to have the nourishment, benefit and support of a hot cooked meal each and every day. That is surely more important than *courtesies*?'

The Reverend Mother's lips tightened. 'I decline to argue with you, Sister Precious. This is only putting distance between us when we — particularly as we are mature sisters — should be closer together, trusting that the Lord will provide. Now, what is the problem? What do you need?'

'Money is what we need. The pantry is almost empty and the fridge is only keeping milk cool.'

'Sister Precious, you know only too well the very great difficulty we have in keeping the convent going since the great depletion in our numbers. But I am determined to do the best I can as mother to keep safe dear Saint Ethel's finger and make this convent acceptable to our Lord and Saviour.'

The Reverend Mother then sat down, pulled open a drawer and produced several twenty-pound notes bound together by an elastic band. She bounced it on the desk. 'Fortunately, the rent was due, so Mr Diamond paid up this morning. God only knows how we shall carry on in the future. But we must do our best. And trust in him. Make that go as far as you can.'

Precious's eyebrows shot up. She reached forward, picked up the money and stuffed it into one of the capacious pockets of her habit. Her face brightened. 'I will be as prudent as I possibly can, Julia.'

'What is Sister Emma working at?'

'I know she was intending to do the laundry,' Precious said.

'That can wait. Take her with you. She can help with the carrying and the lifting.'

'I will.'

A bell rang in the distance.

The Reverend Mother frowned. 'That's the front door.' She frowned. 'Have the front gates not been closed?'

'I think not.'

The Reverend Mother's jaw stiffened. She stood up. 'I must go.'

Precious hurried away, muttering prayers of thanks.

The front door was opening as the Reverend Mother approached it.

A big man in an overcoat and Homburg stepped into entrance hall, put on his best smile, looked round and said, 'Hello, anybody home?'

'I am coming,' the Reverend Mother said.

'My name is Brown, and my associate here is Mr Smith. May we come in, dear lady?'

The Reverend Mother, seeing that he was already in, could only say, 'Of course. What can I do for you?'

The other man, shorter and stockier than his 'associate', entered and closed the door. He stood there with his hat on and his hands in his pockets, looking at his surroundings. The Reverend Mother pursed her lips as she watched him scan the staircase, the ceiling and the walls, peering at pictures of saints and religious scenes on the walls.

'Can I see the manager, the boss, whoever's in charge of the business?' asked Brown.

'That's me. I am the Reverend Mother. How can I help you?'

The man blinked for a second and then said, smiling, 'No, I mean the boss, the man who can make decisions about the security and safety of the girls.'

The Reverend Mother stood her ground. 'I am the . . . erm, boss. I make decisions about everything, most certainly about the safety and well-being of my sisters.'

The man frowned. Then his face suddenly brightened. 'Ah. You'll be the Mother Superior,' he said.

'Well, yes — though in our order we use the name Reverend Mother.'

'We represent the Best Insurance Company. Are your valuables insured, Mother Superior? I know the religious have all sorts of old treasures hidden away in their holy places.'

'On the contrary, Mr Brown, our order takes its vow of poverty quite seriously. We try to grow further in our own spiritual life, of course, try to add in a small way to the quality of life of the local community, but most of all we keep spiritual reverence and guard of the most holy reliquary of the finger of Saint Ethel.'

His eyebrows shot up. 'You are guarding a finger?'

The Reverend Mother nodded. 'The finger of a *saint*.'

'Do you keep it in a vault? Whereabouts do you keep it?'

'We don't have any vaults here. It's in our chapel, in a casket on the altar.'

'Is it all gold, then?'

'No. It is, or it *was* flesh. It is more than eighteen hundred years old.'

With his mouth open, Brown shook his head several times. 'Eighteen hundred years old,' he said.

The Reverend Mother looked at her watch. 'Time is pressing, gentlemen. I have to attend a service shortly. What can I do for you?'

'Well, yes,' the man said, reasserting himself. 'We are in the insurance business, Mother Superior. Supposing you woke up one day and found that the finger had been stolen. How would you feel?'

'I don't think anyone would do such a thing.'

'It could happen. In this day, there are bad people all over the place. Well, you see, for four hundred pounds a month we would ensure that it don't happen. And if it did, we would get it back for you, or one like it.'

She didn't like the turn of the conversation. She looked at her watch again and said, 'The Church pays for our insurance, Mr Brown, such as it is. Now, you must excuse me. I have to go. I have to lead a prayer service at noon.'

As if she hadn't spoken, Brown said, 'The cover is absolutely comprehensive. Thievery, fire, glass breakages, all covered.'

Suddenly there was the sound of breaking glass, and she realised that Smith had used a hammer to smash the frame of a print of Jesus with a dove on his shoulder.

Brown said, 'You see, it could happen, just like that.'

Her eyes flashed and her mouth dropped open. 'May the Lord preserve us.'

Smith applied the hammer to two more large glass-covered prints — Saint Michael surrounded by angels and Mary Magdalene at the tomb.

'And again and again,' Brown said at each hammer blow. 'You need to have a look at your present glass insurance.'

Julia was so distressed she couldn't reply. Instead she dropped to her knees where she was, clenched her hands and closed her eyes. Her lips moved silently and quickly.

Smith looked at her in surprise.

Brown looked at Julia and frowned.

Smith came up him and whispered, 'What do we do now?'

The big man's lips tightened, then he said, 'Shurrup.'

He went up to Julia as she knelt in a praying position, tapped her on the shoulder and said, 'Well . . . er, Mother Superior, think about it. It's only four hundred a month. Fully comprehensive. And you'll be covered for everything. You need the cover to stop more glass damage, possible thievery of that old lady's finger, fire or anything. Imagine this building catching fire. Perhaps some of your ladies dying in the flames and smoke. I shouldn't contact the police, Mother Superior, or you might meet with a very serious accident. We'll be back.'

Brown opened the door and out they went.

THREE

At midday prayers, after the blessing given by Teresa to all the sisters of the convent, the Reverend Mother said, 'My dear sisters, while we are all gathered here, I have an urgent report to give you. I need your confidence, your support, your opinion and your prayers. Please sit down.'

She told them all about the visit that morning from Brown and Smith.

The sisters responded with alarm and cries of outrage and fear.

Then she added, 'We cannot possibly afford to pay them for something we neither need nor want. As it is, we will have to consider how to pay to have the three pictures reglazed. I am positive that the "insurance", as they call it, is purely to satisfy their greed, not their need. However, they threaten that to resist them by reporting it to the police would potentially bring greater trouble upon us.'

'Never mind that, Reverend Mother,' Precious said. 'Report it to the police anyway. It seems that we are in serious trouble whatever we do.'

Some of the others nodded in agreement.

'What? And risk having the blessed finger stolen from us . . . or this beautiful chapel ravaged, our crucifix and altar desecrated? The convent set on fire?'

There were whispered mutterings. One or two of the women made the sign of the cross and bit their lips.

'It's difficult to decide,' Sister Clare said. 'But what could the police do, really? They are as short-staffed as we are. It's a certainty they couldn't be here all the time.'

The Reverend Mother said, 'Nevertheless, I will make a report to the police. Straight after prayers. We must do something. We can't afford to do nothing.'

'It always seems to be a question of money,' Sister Teresa said. 'Reverend Mother, would it not be possible to put the rent of Duxbury Mill up? I have always thought that the rent we are being paid for such an enormous building is not enough.'

'I wish it were possible, Teresa, but I have sought professional advice on this and I understand that we are fortunate to be able to find anyone at all to find commercial use for such a big, old structure. However, that doesn't help the very pressing and worrying situation we find ourselves in *now*.'

Sister Emma, the youngest and prettiest of the sisters, timidly put a hand up to attract Mother's attention. 'We need to pray about this, Reverend Mother, don't we, as well as looking to practical ways?'

'We do indeed, Emma. We will devote our prayers to the insurance men now, and we will devote tonight's prayers at Vespers *and* Compline to them.'

'Let us not panic,' Sister Clare said, 'nor be afraid. Let us rally round the Reverend Mother. She has been personally threatened.' Then she looked at the Reverend Mother and said, 'Even so, Julia, as well as calling on Michael and all the angels in our prayers, we must inform the police and suffer any consequences. On a personal note, I will gladly move my bed into your cell for the time being, if you wish.'

The Reverend Mother stood up. 'Thank you, Clare, but that won't be necessary. But you are absolutely right. I will speak to Inspector Angel. Anything else?' she said as she looked round.

It was a sea of troubled faces.

* * *

'That is about all I can tell you, Inspector.'

'You did right to call us, Reverend Mother,' Angel said.

'We more senior sisters, although not used to being treated to such behaviour and threats, have our faith and spiritual strength to support and defend us, but the younger ones are still building theirs, and I am afraid that they are showing distinct signs of fear of this Mr Brown and Mr Smith. If we were a wealthy convent, we would, I have no doubt, pay them the money. We would be assured that it was the will of God for us to pay them. If the Lord wanted it otherwise he would direct us. But the good Lord is granting us the privilege of having barely enough to pay our own way. We are behind with our electricity bill, our water bill and our candle bill, which keeps our minds, thoughts and concerns in line with most of God's people who are poor, and we are thankful for it.'

Angel thought he understood what the Reverend Mother was saying but could hardly bring himself to think that he could ever be so Christian-like.

'I always thought that the Church was well off, Sister.'

'It is, Inspector, but every unit is expected to be self-supporting — indeed, to contribute to the communal pot. We can't do that. We've not contributed for years. We were and still are dependent on contributions from the community, but since our numbers have dropped, so greatly has our community work . . . visiting, helping, nursing and providing for the poor . . . keeping a high profile — I think that that is what it is called — has not been possible. So benefactors have not come forward. In addition, we have not the numbers to keep our vegetable garden in good order, growing for the needy as well as ourselves.'

Angel sighed gently. 'It's a miracle you survive, Sister.'

'We survive, Inspector, because the convent owns, in perpetuity, Duxbury Mill.'

Angel's face brightened. 'On Sheffield Road.'

The mill was a very big stone building — eight storeys high — which had the word 'Duxbury' on all four sides. Once it had produced cotton textiles, but it had been deserted for many years.

'We are fortunate in having a tenant, Mr Diamond, an entrepreneur, who established a vehicle and bodywork repair business and leases the ground floor from us.'

Angel smiled. 'Good. I'm glad you have something coming in. I'm sorry these villains have caused you so much trouble and pain. Of course you mustn't pay them. Nobody should pay them.

'Now, much as the force detests this kind of offence, if you have no indication as to when they will return, I cannot post personnel here full-time. What we will do is to give you a tiny alarm button, which is on a cord and can be worn round the neck. Press that, and it will trigger the alarm service in the station and play a recorded message that will tell us that you have Brown or Smith on the premises or that they have been in touch. We will respond with all urgency. The message will also be transmitted to my mobile phone, and I will do my best to get here or phone you.'

Julia gave a gentle sigh. 'Oh, that would be good, Inspector.'

Angel smiled. 'And I will arrange for you to be given the alarm button and make the connection straightaway. Now, you know that our patrol cars could be anywhere. One could be passing your door at the very moment you have pressed the button. Of course they may not, but you can be assured that when you have pressed that button, the whole station will be on alert.'

'Thank you very much, Inspector. I have something really hopeful to tell my community.'

* * *

On the night of Thursday, 17 November, round the pubs, snooker halls and wherever men congregate in Bromersley, Angel could be heard: 'I'm looking for a couple of new faces on the insurance racket round here. They're calling themselves Brown and Smith. Heard of them? There's a pony in it for you.'

'Sorry, lad. But I'll ask around,' one man said.

Another said, 'Try the public bar at the Feathers. They're new round here, you said? And they're collar-and-tie wallahs?'

'Yeah,' Angel said.

'There's a lad there, big man, unusual-looking, dark suit, collar and tie. Keeps himself to himself. Drinks Campari. Reads a newspaper.'

'Is his name Smith or Brown?'

'Dunno.'

In a few minutes Angel was in the public bar at the Feathers Hotel. He looked around. It was quite busy. He bought half a bitter and meandered over to the only empty cubicle and sat down. Although he couldn't see everybody in the bar he noticed two men in different cubicles reading. But he was unable to see what they were drinking.

He went out of the bar into the entrance hall, where it was quieter. He took out his mobile and tapped in the number of the Feathers Hotel main switchboard.

It was soon answered.

'The public bar, please,' he said.

'Putting you through.'

A pause. Then, 'Bar manager speaking.'

Angel said, 'Can I speak to Mr Smith, please?'

'There's no Smith here that I know of, sir.'

Angel licked his lips. 'Right, I'll speak to Mr Brown then, please.'

'Which one is that, sir?'

Angel took a chance. 'The one on Campari.'

'Right, sir. I'll get him for you. Hold on.'

Delighted, Angel went back in time to see a big man in a dark suit, collar and tie, carrying a newspaper and a glass of pink liqueur, impatiently pushing his way through a group of men standing and talking and blocking his way to the bar.

The big man picked up the handset. 'Ezra Brown speaking, who is that . . . ? Hello . . . ? Hello? Anybody there . . . ? Hello . . . ?'

Angel smiled, pocketed the mobile, turned and went out of the bar, back through the entrance hall and outside to the car park. He found his car and parked it as close as possible to the front of the hotel. He switched on the car radio for some light music and settled down to wait.

Not long afterwards Ezra Brown came through the swing doors. He stopped on the steps and, using the powerful lights illuminating the front of the hotel, looked at his watch. Angel glanced at the clock in his car automatically. It was 10.55 p.m. Angel noted that the man had a broken nose and appeared to have had some cosmetic work on his top lip which had left him with a cruel, twisted mouth.

Angel took a photograph of Brown with his smartphone. Then he watched him find his car and drive it out of the car park.

It was a big, black American car. Angel took a photograph of it and tapped in the registration number in case there had not been enough light. It was AHE 156.

Then he followed him to the other side of town to a long avenue of large Victorian houses. At the left top corner of the avenue Brown stopped his car unexpectedly. Angel had to slow down quickly and hoped there was a gap in the parked vehicles to give him cover. Luckily there was.

A short, stocky man appeared from behind a post box. He looked round, then quickly opened Brown's car door and climbed in. The car quickly drove off.

From her description, Angel thought that this newcomer might be the Mr Smith that the Reverend Mother had been referring to. Brown drove down the avenue, then halfway down, at number forty-five, he turned into the small driveway.

Angel slowed and pulled into the kerb. He switched off the engine and wondered what to do next. He noticed that there seemed to be no pedestrians around. There was the occasional car passing by.

Moments later, Brown's car came back into the avenue, closely followed by a much older big American car driven by the stocky man. Angel noted that car's registration number, CYR 253. They drove in convoy to the town centre, Angel keeping well behind. Brown drove round a block in the town centre, then, unexpectedly, started to make the same circuit again. He sped round to the front of the Bromersley Building Society while Angel began to make the turn, when suddenly, like an icicle dropping down the back of his neck, Angel realised he was in trouble. He stopped his car. A repeated run round the same block of buildings would have indicated to Brown that he was following them. Any second would come the payoff. He wasn't intending to wait for it.

It was too late.

He caught sight of shadows in his mirror.

They were on foot . . . creeping up on him in the dark.

He quickly started his car and drove away.

Hot lead rattled on the car bodywork as Smith and Brown fired off several rounds.

Angel was surprised that they were armed with guns. It put a whole new perspective on their activities, and greatly motivated him to get away from them at speed. He drove in a zigzag route including turning up a one-way street the wrong way and driving over two pedestrian-only walkways to get out of their range — luckily, the streets were deserted at this time of night. He kept up the speed until he considered he was safe, then he parked in a line of cars at the side of the road and switched off the lights.

In the dark he opened the glove compartment of the dashboard and fished around among handcuffs, ballpoint pens, sunglasses, dusters and paperclips and smiled when he found what he was looking for. It was an L-shaped piece of copper piping. He put that in his jacket pocket. Then he checked the time. It was a quarter past midnight. Probably too late to phone Mary and tell her he'd be late. She'd likely have fallen asleep. He wouldn't want to wake her up to tell her the obvious.

He started the car and drove it as quietly as he could back towards the town centre and parked it two streets from the block of shops and offices where Smith and Brown had fired at him.

He walked as quietly as he could towards the Bromersley Building Society and the Northern Bank. He got to a corner where he could peep round and see if anything was happening. The main street was well illuminated from street lights, advertising signs and shop window displays.

He could see that the big, older car that had been driven by Smith was positioned at the far end on the main road about three hundred metres away, with the front facing Melvyn Minter's little newsagent's. The car doors were open and the man he'd assumed was Smith was leaning into the car. Angel frowned as he tried to understand what they were doing.

Angel looked round. He couldn't see Brown anywhere.

He couldn't miss this opportunity. He reached into his pocket for the piece of bent copper tubing, then tiptoed the short distance to the car, pushed the pipe end hard into Smith's lower back and said, in his best, slow, silky whisper, 'Put your hands in the air and stand up *very, very* slowly.'

Smith stiffened. 'All right. All right,' he said quickly. 'I'll do whatever you say.'

'Close the door. Put your hands on the roof of the car.'

The man obeyed instantly.

Angel patted him down with his free hand. He felt a small gun in the jacket pocket and took it out. Even in the bad light, he could see that the gun was a .32 Beretta Tomcat. It was ready for action: it had a bullet 'up the spout'. He reached in through the open door of the old car and pushed the gun into the corner leather upholstery of the back seat so that it couldn't be seen. Then, feeling much relieved that he had one deadly weapon out of the way, he pressed the copper pipe harder into Smith's back.

'Right, now, what are you up to?'

'Nuthin',' Smith said.

'It's the middle of the night. Why aren't you neatly tucked up in bed with your teddy bear?'

'Couldn't sleep.'

'Where's your friend Brown?'

'Dunno.'

Then suddenly, he felt a gun in his back and a voice behind him said, 'I'm here, right behind you. Put your hands up. Don't turn round.'

Then to Smith, Brown said, 'Quick. Get his gun, Reg.'

Smith looked at Angel's hand and gasped. 'Eh? He hasn't got one! A bit of tubing.'

'Where's yours?'

'I don't know. He took it.'

Then Angel felt something heavy hit him at the back of his head. His eyes closed. He slumped down in the road. He saw bubbles escaping from a big bubble, and then bubbles escaping from those bubbles and so on and then black . . . then nothing.

* * *

Down a tunnel Angel heard a woman's voice say, 'I think he's coming round.'

And then a man said, 'What's his name, nurse?'

There were some faint clattering sounds. 'Erm . . . It's on his notes . . . Michael, I think. Yes. Michael.'

'Wake up, Michael,' the man said. 'Come on. You're all right, Michael. Come on.'

Angel opened his eyes, and found that he was being stared at by a young man in blue hospital theatre clothes with a stethoscope round his neck.

The young man smiled.

Behind him Angel saw a nurse holding a file of papers. She was also smiling.

He looked around. His was the only bed in the tiny ward. He tried to sit up but the doctor stopped him. 'You're all right there, Michael. Stay still. I'm a doctor. Firstly, I need to know if you're in any pain.'

Angel thought a moment. 'No.'

'Particularly in the head?'

'No.'

'Are your eyes all right? Any double vision?'

'No.'

The doctor nodded. 'You were found in the road in the centre of Bromersley. How did you arrive there? Had you been drinking?'

'Certainly not. I'm a police inspector. I was in the business of detaining a man when I was hit at the back of my head with something heavy. I don't know what it was.'

'You do have a contusion on the back of your head. Then what happened?'

'I woke up here just now. Did anybody make an arrest?'

'I really don't know,' the doctor said. Then he stood up, glanced at the nurse, sorted his notes and added, 'Well, that's all for now. Get some rest and I'll look in tomorrow.'

Angel couldn't believe it. 'But I feel all right,' he said. 'I must get out. I've a lot of work to catch up on.'

'Oh no,' the doctor said, smiling at the nurse as he made for the door. 'Far too early to think about returning to work. Let's see what you're like in the morning.'

'But Doctor!' Angel protested.

The door closed quickly. He was gone.

The nurse came up quickly. 'There's a lady asking to see you. A Miss Flora Carter. Is she a relation?'

Angel was pleased. 'No,' he said at first, then he thought it could be that Flora wouldn't be allowed to visit him if she *wasn't* a relation, so he quickly said, 'Yes. Yes, she's my . . . wife. My live-in wife. I mean my partner.'

'You can see her for a few minutes.'

Detective Sergeant Flora Carter had a lot to say.

'There's a bit of a flap on at the station,' she said. 'In the early hours of this morning an old car was driven into a little newsagent's on King Street. We've had to close the street to traffic. At first it looked like a freak accident, but Inspector Asquith found a brick tied with string on the accelerator pedal.'

Angel rubbed his chin. It must have been intentional, then, he thought. But what's the motive?

'Anybody hurt, Flora? Anything stolen? Is there much damage?'

'Nobody hurt, sir. Nothing worth stealing . . . only magazines and books. But the shopfront . . . it was only small, you know, sir. That's all gone, and the doorway. And there's damage to the walls of both the building society and the bank.'

'And the car?'

'That's a write-off.'

'I have a particular interest in that old car, Flora. Keep track of it. It'll have to be moved. I must know *where* the wreck is. Before it is moved, have the usual checks made, fingerprints, photographs, position measured relating to everything else. You know what's wanted. Then have the wreck brought to the station pound.'

'Right, sir.'

Then he said, 'Will you do a check on a couple of car registrations for me? They are CYR 253, that's the car in the crash, and AHE 156. I expect they'll be false, but who knows.'

DS Carter wrote them in her notebook. 'Got them, sir.'

Angel frowned. 'Any sign of the shopkeeper?'

'He's been and gone. Very distressed by all the damage. I've got his name and address.' She turned back several pages of her notebook. 'Ah, here it is. Melvyn Minter, 5 Church Walk.'

Angel consigned it to his memory.

'Something else, Flora, while I remember. My car is parked in the centre of town . . . on a little road off King Street, on the south side . . . not far from the incident. Will you rescue it?'

The nurse came in. She stood at the door feigning surprise at the presence of Flora Carter. 'You still here?' Then she looked at Angel. 'Another lady is here to see you. She says *she's* Mrs Angel!'

FOUR

Angel had avoided serious concussion and the doctor was happy to discharge him from the hospital the following morning.

He made his way to the police station straightaway. He had to report in to the office of his immediate superior and CEO of the station, Detective Superintendent Horace Harker.

Angel wrinkled his nose, made his way up the corridor to the last door but one, tapped on it and went in.

The office was untidy, overheated and smelled of menthol. It was always like that.

DS Harker was not immediately visible. He was seated at his desk behind several piles of letters, files, reports, books and boxes of pills and bottles of medicine or ointment. In boring moments, Angel tried to read the labels of some of them. There were pills for arthritis, headache, coughs and colds, upset stomach, diarrhoea, constipation, haemorrhoids, gout . . . and complaints he could neither pronounce nor spell.

Harker's head was the shape of a turnip. He was mostly bald but had a collar of white hair.

He popped up behind his desk between piles of files and papers and said irritably, 'Well, sit down, Angel. There. Opposite me. Where I can see you. That's it.'

Angel sat down on the only chair his side of the desk.

It was only a matter of minutes before they were in a heated discussion about a controversial subject.

'. . . And that's why I am asking for temporary permission to carry a firearm, sir,' Angel said.

'You know full well that that's not allowed,' Harker said. 'And the circumstances you outline do not warrant a suspension of the rule. As you know, you can call on Wakefield's armed unit, who are always on standby to support you if you find yourself facing or about to face armed suspects.'

'Yes sir, but in most situations the need for a firearm is required at that moment. There is no time to phone Wakefield then wait thirty minutes or so for them to arrive with their submachine guns. A dozen or more innocent people — witnesses — could be murdered in that time and the villains will have escaped.'

'You're painting the very worst scenario, Angel. The answer must still be no. I don't make the law. Nor do you. It's our job to keep the law, not break it because it's inconvenient or difficult. Sadly, much of our work includes dealing with armed villains.'

Angel thought a moment. 'But sir, on the occasions that we have a case where a villain is known to be armed, for the sake of the life of the investigating police officer, could an exception not be made?'

Harker's face tightened. 'You can reword the question and make it as emotive as you like,' he said, 'but the answer is still no.'

Angel wrinkled his nose.

Harker continued, 'And it would be no use going over my head to see the chief constable. He fully understands the law of the land and the conditions in which a person may own a firearm and he fully supports them. We are in complete agreement on that subject.'

Angel sighed. 'Well, sir, I say this respectfully. I sincerely hope that neither you nor the chief constable ever have to face a man with a gun who may have murdered before and therefore has nothing to lose.'

Harker's eyes widened. Pointing a finger at Angel, he said, 'I have no more time to waste arguing the point with you, Angel. I have some important work to do. I have to find a Father Christmas for the children's Christmas party. The usual man has retired.'

Angel threw up his hands in dismay. He came out of Harker's office and silently ran through every expletive he could think of all the way down to his own office. He banged the door and slumped down in his chair. He sighed noisily then ran his hand through his hair. He couldn't miss the new pile of post and reports on his desk right in front of him. It was quite difficult to believe that a pile that big had only accumulated over two days. He glared at it, then violently pushed it all off the desk on to the floor.

It was at that point that the office door opened. It was DS Flora Carter. She had a handful of envelopes and packets in her hand.

'Sorry, sir, I didn't know you were in.' She saw the letters, packages and reports littered across the floor. 'Having a tidy-up, sir?' She looked up at him, and the smile melted off her face. 'What's happened?'

He looked at her coldly and didn't reply.

'I've got today's post, sir,' she said, holding it out to him.

'Put it on the floor,' he said.

She frowned and then placed the pile on the desk directly in front of him.

With a swift sweep of the arm he pushed that off the edge of the desk and on to the floor to join the rest.

Carter's eyes and mouth momentarily opened wide. Then she frowned.

'Are you all right, sir?'

'No, Flora,' he said very deliberately. 'I am not all right.'

'Why don't you ring your GP?'

'I don't need a doctor.'

'Are you sure?'

'I'm feeling better already. Flora, can I ask you something?'

She nodded. 'Yes, of course.'

'You presently live at home with your mum and dad . . . and you get on well with them . . . you love them, don't you?'

'Yes, sir. Very much.'

'Good. Say a man came into your house with a gun and threatened to shoot the three of you. What would you do? Would you expect your father to take the initiative in trying to save the three of you, or your mother . . . or yourself?'

'What a question.'

'Purely hypothetical.'

Lines appeared across her forehead as she considered an answer. 'Well, I suppose I would try to take the initiative, sir. Mother is out of it. And Dad's too old to be involved in any sort of an argument with a man with a gun.'

'Good,' Angel said. 'And I believe that — in your circumstances — that is absolutely the right attitude. That's all. I feel all right now, Flora. Absolutely.'

'You don't look it.'

'I am. I am. Really, I am.'

'If you are sure . . . ?'

'*Yes*. Did you want anything else?'

'You asked me to check on two vehicle registration numbers,' Carter said. 'CYR 253 and AHE 156.'

'Yes.'

'They were both duff.'

Angel nodded. It was as expected.

'Put the AHE one on the wanted list to report to me when and where it is seen *immediately*, but do not apprehend. Say the passengers will be armed. I don't want any deaths.'

Carter blinked and sucked in some air. 'Are they armed?'

'To their *teeth*.'

Carter shuddered. 'Going to have to be careful, then.' She turned to go, then she turned back. 'Your car is in the pound, sir. So is the wreck you were interested in.'

Angel's eyebrows went up. When Carter had gone, he promptly went out of the office and made his way past the cells, through the rear entrance to the police car park and behind that the pound.

He immediately spotted his own car and saw that next to it was the wreck, with its front wheels splayed at unusual angles and the bonnet and radiator compressed and broken up.

He went straight up to the wreck. He opened the rear off-side door, reached into the upholstery in the corner of the car and pulled out the Beretta he had taken from the villain, Smith.

He looked round. Nobody was about. He quickly pushed it into his pocket.

He immediately felt a warm, comfortable glow in his chest.

He was pleased but not excessively. He also felt guilty because it was clearly against the law and the rules of an institution that was dear to him. However, taking everything into consideration, he reckoned he could live with that now that he had balanced the power a little between the Ezra Brown gang and himself.

He intended to live a long and full life.

* * *

He returned to his office, saw the mess of letters and other paperwork on the floor, pulled a face of resignation, then crouched down and began to gather them up.

The phone rang.

He stood up. Picked up the handset.

'Angel,' he said.

It was the civilian woman on the police station exchange. 'Inspector, I have a man on the line wanting to speak to you. He won't give his name. He says it's very important. Will you speak to him?'

'Yes, of course. Put him through, please.' He reached across the desk to switch on the recording machine.

'Are you Inspector Angel?' the caller said.

The voice was that of a local man, educated but not necessarily an academic.

'Yes. Who is that?'

'Are you looking for a Mr Brown?'

'Yes.'

'He'd like to meet you. He has a very interesting proposition he wishes to put to you. He asks if you'll you meet him at 129 Huddersfield Road at eight o'clock tonight.'

'Very well. I'll be very interested to hear what he has to say.'

'Come alone, and no tricks,' the caller said, and ended the call.

Angel slowly put the phone back in its holster.

He sat in the chair, put his elbows on the desk and spread his fingers at each side of his head. It was one of his thinking positions. After a while he took out his mobile. He scrolled down to a phone number and clicked on it.

'Can you come in for a minute?' he said.

When DS Carter arrived he told her what had happened and played the recording.

'And what are you going to do, sir?'

'I will meet him, but I don't trust him, Flora. It's hard to believe that he thinks I would be corrupt enough that they could buy me off.'

'You mean a bribe?'

'If it isn't that, I can't think what else he might want to say. It'll not be to give himself up, you can bet on that. At around seven thirty tonight I want you to discreetly go up there, park up and observe. But take care, Flora — he will be carrying a gun and you won't be.'

'Right,' she said.

'I am going up there now to have a look.'

* * *

Angel drove his car past 129 Huddersfield Road, moving quickly in case he was being observed. There was a poster in the bay window advertising that the house was for sale. It was a large end-terrace stone-fronted house built in the 1920s. It was on the corner of a narrow street that led to more houses. There was a lamppost on the corner.

There were a few cars parked along the road. He couldn't see any drivers or passengers inside them. The pavements were empty. There were no pedestrians at all. There were a few vehicles travelling in either direction. He turned round after half a mile, returned and parked the car outside number 129. He got out and glanced around. He opened the gate and walked up the path, past the small, slightly neglected garden, to the front steps. There were three steep stone steps up to the door. He pressed the bell push and banged the knocker. There was no reply. He peered through the letterbox. There was no furniture in the hall. He took the opportunity to turn round and observe the road and the lamppost from the top step. Then he looked at the poster in the bay window to record the name and phone number of the estate agent selling the house. It was an old established Bromersley firm. He noticed that that room was clear of furniture. The entire house must be empty.

He drove solemnly back to the police station. Then he phoned the estate agent, introduced himself and told the agent he was making police enquiries about the property, and that he wasn't a potential buyer.

'Who is the vendor?'

'An old lady who lived there many years, but she said she couldn't manage a house that size anymore and her son has taken her to live with him in Carlisle,' the agent said.

'How long has the house been unoccupied?'

'Only a week or so.'

'Have you had much interest?'

'We always get a lot of time wasters at first in a house of that quality, but I reckon we've had two serious enquiries.'

'Have you their names and addresses?'

'I'm digging them out for you now. One enquiry was from a young professional couple. They liked it but they were worried about getting a mortgage. The other interested party was a man. Didn't say much.'

Angel's forehead wrinkled and his eyelids came halfway down. 'What was his name?'

'I'm just looking it up, Inspector . . . won't keep you a second . . . here we are. His name's Brown.'

On hearing the name, Angel's pulse rate increased. He gently sighed and blew out a length of air. 'And have you got his address?'

'He didn't leave one. He said he was always on the move. And that if he wanted to go any further with the purchase, he would phone back.'

It was the answer Angel expected.

'If he calls back, please let me know. It's very important.'

He ended the call but hung on to the phone, sat back in his chair and rubbed his chin. After a minute or so, he tapped an internal number on to the pad.

A young male voice answered. 'Stores and armoury.'

'Is that PC John Sellars?'

'Yes, sir.'

'I want to see you, John.'

'I'll come up right away, sir.'

* * *

After a snack at the pub, Angel went direct to 5 Church Walk and pressed the doorbell.

The door was opened by a woman in her sixties. Her eyes were red and holding a tissue.

Angel said, 'Mrs Minter?'

'Yes?'

'I'm from the police.' He showed her his warrant card. 'Inspector Angel.'

She looked both surprised and relieved. 'Come in,' she said.

'It's a Mr Melvyn Minter I would like to see.'

'That's my husband, Inspector. I'm afraid he's in bed. He's not very well. He's hardly eating anything. He has a cup of tea now and then. He sleeps through the day but is wide awake all night long. I don't want to disturb him, unless it's very urgent.'

Angel's eyebrows shot up. 'I'm sorry to hear that. Has he been ill long?'

'No, it came on quite sudden. It was after some trouble he had at the shop last Tuesday morning.'

Angel said, 'What sort of trouble?'

'Hasn't he reported it to you? He said he would.'

Angel shook his head and said, 'No, not that I'm aware.'

Mrs Minter then revealed to Angel all that her husband had told her about that Tuesday. Then she went on to explain that the old car made to run into the front of their shop was the execution of a threat made on that day.

'If your husband had promptly reported to us all that you have just told me, we would have been able to prevent your shop being smashed up. And we may have been in a position to arrest the two men as well.'

'My husband is not a strong man, Inspector. And he was afraid of reprisals.'

'Of course he was,' Angel said. 'That's how these crooks work. Terror is their byword.'

'And they have won,' she said. 'They've put us out of business . . . taken our only source of income. Melvyn will never get a job at his age. To tell the truth, Inspector, the shop was hardly keeping us as it was. Now with all that damage, we can't afford to pay for a new shopfront and door and a few thousand or more on replacement stock. And we certainly couldn't afford four hundred pounds a month so-called insurance. I expect that's the going rate for them. Mrs Levi said that that's what her husband is paying. Well *we* couldn't afford to pay it.'

At the mention of Mrs Levi's name, Angel's interest was piqued. 'Who is Mrs Levi?'

Mrs Minter seemed suddenly crestfallen. 'Oh dear. You didn't know? Perhaps I shouldn't have mentioned the name.'

'If it is anything to do with these crooks you most certainly should have told me. Did you say that Mr Levi is paying these crooks?'

She nodded.

'And has Mr Levi a business?'

'Oh dear,' she said, not knowing what to do with her hands.

'Has Mr Levi a business?'

'Yes. He has that antiques shop on the corner of Scargill Street and Market Street. Please don't tell them I told you.'

Angel smiled. 'Don't worry. I won't.'

The door opened and a man's head with ruffled hair peered through. 'I thought I heard voices,' he said.

Mrs Minter saw him and stood up. 'Are you all right, Melvyn?' she said. 'Come and sit down. I'll make you some tea.'

'I don't want anything,' Minter said.

She put up a protesting hand and made for the kitchen.

Mr Minter came into the room. He was dressed in striped pyjamas and looked thin and pale.

'Who are you?' he asked.

'I am Inspector Angel from Bromersley police. I came to see you. As you were asleep, I have been talking to your wife.'

Minter looked towards the kitchen and called, 'And what have you been telling him?'

'What *you* said *you* had told him,' she called back.

Minter moaned, slumped down on the settee and put his hands up to his face. 'Not only are we bankrupt, she's now put our lives in jeopardy.'

'No she hasn't, Mr Minter. Those crooks will not be back. You've just said you're bankrupt. That means you have nothing. They aren't interested in people who have nothing. They can't rob people who have nothing, can they?' Angel said.

He waited for a reply.

'Can they?' Angel repeated.

Eventually it came.

'They can take our lives,' Minter whispered.

'What use is that to them?'

'For revenge.'

'They've had their revenge. They had it when they ran that old car into your shopfront. They will move on. There are millions of other innocent, honest people who have money that they can try their dishonourable tricks on. The damage to your shop is their revenge and a threat to other reluctant innocents.'

Minter removed his hands from his face.

'Do you really think so?' he said.

'I *know* so.'

Minter looked at Angel with a glimmer of hope in his eyes.

Angel said, 'You need to concentrate your mind on either rebuilding the business you already have and know about, or seek employment elsewhere. I realise that your age will be against you, but there are vacancies all over, you might find a slot that fits your experience, such as shop manager. You may have to start as a shelf filler in a supermarket. But there are jobs all over. Don't assume you won't find anything.'

Mrs Minter came in carrying a tray of tea things. 'And I can go back to work too. That'll be two wage packets coming in.'

'I don't want my wife to start going out to work again at her age,' Minter said.

She looked at Angel. 'He keeps saying that.'

'Why ever not?' Angel said. 'Most women go out to work these days. More than half of MPs' spouses — that's both women and men — are fully employed in businesses, law or politics. Many of them will be over sixty years of age. They're not too proud to earn money.'

Minter sat upright on the settee. He looked brighter than he had ever looked.

'Really?' he said. He looked at his wife. 'Did you hear that, love?'

Mrs Minter nodded. 'I told you that, but you never listen.' Then she turned back to the tray she was holding. 'I've made us all a cup of tea.'

She stirred a beaker and passed it to her husband. 'Melvyn,' she said.

'Thank you, love,' he said. 'Is there any food going?'

She smiled, glanced at Angel, looked back at her husband and said, 'What do you want?'

'A big fry-up,' he said, licking his lips.

FIVE

After Angel asked a few questions about Brown and Smith, he took his leave of the Minters and went straight round to Scargill Street to Levi's Antiques.

As Angel opened the shop door it tapped a big coiled spring fastened to a bell hanging just above the door.

It was a small shop but brimming with old pots, huge vases, glassware, glass showcases and old furniture. He noticed that the front of one of the large glass display cases had had a recent blow at one point, a crack that had spread in all directions like an irregular star. At that time, the shop had no customers.

A thin young man with a short jet-black beard and receding hair was behind the counter. He leaned forward and smiled.

Angel flashed his warrant card in front of the young man's face. 'Inspector Angel, Bromersley police. Are you Mr Levi?'

'I am.'

'Do you mind if I ask, are you the only person who serves here?'

'I am almost always here. My wife helps on Fridays and Saturdays, when we are busier. Why do you ask?'

'We're calling on all businesspeople to warn them of the possible approach of two men who call themselves Brown and Smith, supposedly selling insurance. It's a scam, of course. The insurance is grossly overpriced. And it's insurance from the damage *they* do or *threaten* to do that one actually needs.'

Angel looked into Levi's face. He didn't even blink.

Angel continued. 'They usually start demanding a payment of four hundred pounds a month, but then as time goes by they bump it up to whatever amount they think the poor victim will pay.'

Levi's expression still didn't change.

'They use bullying and terrifying methods to extract the money,' Angel said. 'If you don't conform, they increase their wickedness. You'll know that they've closed down Minter's Magazine shop.'

'Yes. That's outrageous. You're a policeman, why don't you arrest them?'

'We would if we knew where they were, or where they were going to be. We need someone who perhaps is "insured" with them and paying them money regularly to step forward and assist us. Until we put those two crooks behind bars, this will continue. It needs someone with intelligence, foresight and bravery.'

Levi was giving nothing away.

Angel stood back from the counter and pointed to the large showcase with the damaged glass. 'That's a mess. How did that happen?'

Mr Levi's eyes flashed. Panic showed in his face.

'Erm . . . erm . . . a woman bumped into it with a push-chair,' he said.

'It's just the sort of damage that Brown and Smith do when they're not getting their own way.' Angel looked into Levi's eyes and slowly said, 'Are you *sure* you haven't been approached by them?'

Levi looked away. Then suddenly he looked back at Angel. 'Oh, Inspector . . . they threatened to set fire to the shop . . .'

His eyes were moist, his voice unsteady and his hands shaking.

'Since then, I have been out of my mind worrying about the safety of my wife and our children. You see, we live upstairs and—'

'So you are paying Brown and Smith every month?'

'Ye-ye-yes.'

Angel smiled. 'Well, rejoice, Mr Levi. There's no need to worry any more. And you don't have to pay them any longer. When is your next so-called premium due?'

'Next Monday. The twenty-first.'

'Good.' Angel nodded slowly. 'And how is the money paid?'

'Either Smith or Brown or both of them call. It's four hundred pounds in cash.'

'If we haven't caught them by then, I'll be back early on Monday morning.'

Angel was hopeful that his meeting with Brown that night might result in the crooks' arrest. In which case, nobody would be calling to take the money from Mr Levi next Monday.

* * *

When Angel returned to his office, on his desk there was a big plastic bag. Tacked to it was a note which read, 'DI Angel. I think these will be a good fit on you. John Sellars, PC. Duty armourer.'

Inside the bag were two heavy navy-blue pads. One was the approximate shape of the chest and stomach area from the neck down to the groin, and the other one the approximate area for the back. They fastened to each other by leather straps and buckles over the shoulders and under the arms.

Angel held the front piece in front of him. He nodded and put it back on the desk.

Then he picked up the phone and tapped in a two-digit number. 'Will you find DC Scrivens and tell him I want him?'

Then he tapped in another two-digit number. 'I want to speak to Inspector Haydn Asquith . . . Yes, I'll hold . . . Ah, Haydn. Look, I know it's Friday, but could I possibly borrow Patrolman Sean Donohue for two hours, no more, tonight . . . No, but . . . I didn't know. No, all right. I'll manage somehow . . . I understand, Haydn. All right. Bye.'

He wrinkled his nose, and rubbed his forehead with the fingers and thumb of one hand.

There was a knock at the door.

'Come in.'

It was DC Ted Scrivens.

'Ah, sit down, Ted. I want you to do a bit of overtime tonight.'

* * *

It was 7.50 p.m. that Friday evening when Angel, having fastened his shirt buttons over the body armour with difficulty, took the Beretta Tomcat out of his pocket, checked that the cassette was full, that there was a bullet up the spout and that the safety catch was on. Satisfied, he pushed it back into his pocket.

Five minutes later, he pulled away from Bromersley Police Station to keep his appointment to see the man known as Ezra Brown at the big empty house at the west side of town.

There was very little traffic about . . . a couple of delivery vans and no pedestrians.

As he drew near to 129 Huddersfield Road, he saw that three cars were parked close together against the kerb on the left-hand side of the road forty metres from the house. He felt a little comforted to see DS Flora Carter's unmarked car between the two of them.

There were no lights coming from the inside of the house.

He parked his car outside the front of the house. He checked his watch. It was exactly eight o'clock.

He got out of the car, walked up the path to the top step and banged the knocker on the front door.

Although the house was still in darkness, the lamp on the corner abundantly illuminated the garden, the path, the door and Angel.

There was still no reply. He banged the knocker harder and for longer.

Then he heard a car engine on the main road behind him. He turned to see a car heading in his direction. As it got nearer it increased speed.

Angel's pulse began to thump.

It looked like Brown's car.

The number plate was AHE 156.

It *was* Brown's car.

Angel could see the driver's window was down, and the next thing he heard was the sound of shooting. As he turned away he felt two hits in his back. He leapt across the garden and jumped over the wall on to the pavement about two metres down. Then he ran up the side road and kept running. Everywhere were houses. He heard the car engine behind him. He found a low wall in a private garden in front of a house and hid behind it. His heart pounded and he thanked his maker for the body armour he was wearing.

He saw headlights illuminating the street. The engine sounded louder. The car came level with him and was only four metres away. It wasn't travelling fast. The light wasn't good enough there to see the driver or any other figures. He couldn't even see if the car windows were open or not. He took out the Beretta and aimed it at the nearside front window. He pulled the trigger. There was the sound of a shot and the shattering of glass.

The car instantly picked up speed and raced away into the darkness.

Angel took the opportunity to change his position in readiness for any subsequent attack. He ran further up the street until he was panting like a Labrador. There were two wheelie bins on the corner pavement. One of them was overfull. The lid hung down, and paper and plastic packing was heaped to overflowing. In the dim light, at the top he saw a dark plastic bag. It had the M & S logo printed in black across the middle of it. It looked clean. He had a use for that. He quickly folded it and shoved it in his pocket. Then he bobbed down and hid behind the bins. Just in time.

He saw the beam of another car and heard the sound of its engine. It was different from Brown's. In the dim light, he could make out the silhouette of the car and recognised it as Carter's.

She had been briefed to follow Brown's car, leapfrogging with Scrivens until Brown arrived at his destination, then to return to the station.

Angel remained hidden behind the wheelie bins to avoid confusing her.

Carter's car rushed past, followed by Scrivens in a Ford Escort.

Angel still kept his head down until the car passed. He was pleased that the plan seemed to be working. He waited a minute or so. He listened out for any other car engine and looked round for any headlights that might be coming his way . . . but there was nothing.

He quickly retraced his steps back down the street to the house and to his car. Then he phoned up Carter on his mobile. He was interested to hear where Brown was heading, but he was also concerned for her safety.

'Can you talk, Flora?'

'Yes, sir.'

'Where are you? Are you safe?'

'I'm fine. I'm in the centre of town. On King Street. I believe I've lost Brown.'

Angel pulled an unhappy face. 'Oh. Be careful, Flora. Watch out that he's not behind you. Are you in touch with Ted Scrivens?'

'No. I was earlier. But I haven't seen him in my mirror for a while.'

Angel sighed. Things were not going well. 'I'll check in with him and come back to you soon, Flora.'

He closed the call and scrolled to Scrivens number.

'Where are you, Ted?'

'On the road to Huddersfield. I'm about three miles out of Bromersley.'

Angel's heart missed a beat. 'Spotted Brown's car?'

'I'm behind it. Trying not to be obvious. I could do with a changeover. He'll spot me for certain soon.'

Angel had to think quickly. His first instinct was to follow Scrivens and continue the surveillance, but his own car was known to Brown.

'Ted,' he said, 'next time Brown makes an obvious turning, you go straight on or turn in the opposite direction. All right?'

Scrivens gasped. 'But if I do that, we'll lose him, sir!'

'I would rather lose him than lose you. He has a firearm. You haven't. He's wanted for a long list of offences. He's a desperate man. Do as I tell you.'

Angel pressed the cancel button and scrolled down to Carter.

'Yes, sir?' she said.

'Ah, Flora. I'm in my car on Huddersfield Road. Come quickly and pick me up. We're going to find Ted Scrivens.'

Seven minutes later, Angel was driving Carter's car and speeding along in the direction of Huddersfield. Fortunately, at that time of night the roads were not busy and Angel knew the way well enough.

He glanced at Carter. 'Ring Ted Scrivens and let's see how he's doing.'

Scrivens's voice came over the car speakers. 'Brown's car turned left on to a farmer's track . . . I'm not sure if it isn't unclassified . . . so I went straight on a hundred metres or so towards Huddersfield. Now I'm on the main road opposite the Cat and the Fiddle pub.'

Angel said, 'I know it. We'll meet you there in a few minutes.'

He pressed his foot down harder on the accelerator pedal and the car surged forward.

He ended the call, then to Carter he said, 'Look at the map, Flora. See if there is a track or a lane before the Cat and the Fiddle on the left.'

'There is, sir. It's called Vesty's Lane. It leads through a big area of farmland to a set of buildings called Vesty's Hall. Then the lane continues a short way to another much smaller building, Vesty's Lodge.'

'Oh?' Angel licked his lips in hopeful expectation. 'Is that a dead end?'

'No sir. It continues a little way then joins up with a network of lanes that lead all over.'

He ran his hand through his hair then rubbed the back of his neck. 'That means that Brown could live *anywhere*!'

'Afraid so.'

Angel pulled a disagreeable face and returned to concentrating on his driving.

A few minutes later, he said, 'We're coming to the Cat and the Fiddle, Flora. Look out for Ted Scrivens. He said he was parked opposite.'

'He's there, sir,' she said as the car headlights shone directly on the man, causing him to shield his eyes.

Scrivens was at the side of the road, standing against the little Ford Escort.

Angel stopped and lowered the car window as Scrivens ran up to it.

'That lane leads to a place called Vesty's Hall, Ted. Let's have a look at it. Approach very quietly. I'll follow you.'

'Right, sir,' Scrivens said, and rushed off to his car.

In convoy, they drove along the straight, flat road, which cut through a huge ploughed area for a mile or so to a complex of old buildings comprising a large house with farm outbuildings, several trees and small areas of grass.

They followed as far as a sign that said: 'Vesty's Hall. NO ENTRY. Private Property. Enquiries Vesty's Estates Office, Huddersfield.' It was attached to a large aluminium gate with barbed wire wound with big loops across the top of it.

As Angel drew up behind him, Scrivens got out of the car and went back to meet him.

Angel also got out for a better look at the old buildings in the moonlight. He saw that the front door and the windows on the south and west sides of the big house were boarded up.

He went up to the big gate and shone his torch on the hinges. They were well oiled. He then went to the other end of the gate. Carefully threading his hand through loops of barbed wire, he found the latch and easily lifted it. That also was well oiled and wasn't locked.

He turned back to Scrivens. 'I'm just going to have a quick look round.'

Angel slipped quietly into the yard and surveyed some of the outhouses. There were no vehicles, but tyre marks and the smell of petrol left him in no doubt that some of them had been used as garages recently.

He walked round the outside of the house and found all the windows and doors were boarded up. He couldn't find any footprints or giveaway signs that the house was being lived in.

Angel was tired and not very happy. 'Brown's not here,' he said. 'Let's press on.'

They made their way back to the lane and drove towards Vesty's Lodge.

* * *

A small man with long hair and a beard climbed down from the rafters of one of the outbuildings of the big house and rushed out to the gate. Peering out between the bars at the two vehicles on the lane in the moonlight, he scowled, showing teeth like a piano keyboard. He pulled out a cell phone and made a call.

Three minutes after that, Brown's car, complete with Brown, Smith and two hastily packed suitcases, shot out of the very short lane from Vesty's Lodge and turned left on to the main track through the ploughed area.

* * *

'The lodge is all lit up, sir,' Scrivens's voice came over the radio. 'And the gate's wide open.'

Angel's eyebrows shot up. 'There must be somebody in there,' he said. 'We'll leave our cars here, Ted, and go on foot. Stay here with the cars, Flora. If we're not back in ten minutes, send for backup.'

Angel and Scrivens walked quickly and quietly into the yard. Vesty's Lodge was a small stone house; the windows and the front door were boarded up. They walked around to the back and saw that, although in the past someone had boarded it up, some strips of board had been torn off the back door. The door was slightly ajar, light shining through the gap.

Angel pushed the door wide open. They went inside on tiptoe. The room was a kitchen, lit by a bare bulb in the ceiling. It was tidy and clean, but there was no sign of life. There were two doors. He opened one. It was a pantry, almost empty. Scrivens opened the other door. It was a room in darkness. He found the light switch, and discovered a deserted living room and a set of creaking stairs.

Upstairs, they found a bathroom and two bedrooms, but again, no sign of Brown and company. The bathroom was in darkness and the bedrooms had the lights on. The beds were unmade . . . just an untidy heap of old blankets, and there was the minimum of furniture. Angel saw a newspaper on the uncarpeted floor sticking out from under one of the beds. He leaned down and picked it up. It was a copy of the *Bromersley Chronicle*, a local weekly paper, dated last Friday, 11 November, and folded to a page that had a neat rectangular hole in it where something had been cut out. It was among the classified advertisements . . . single column about three centimetres long. Angel rolled up the paper and stuffed it into his pocket.

'I don't think there's anything more here, Ted.'

'The birds have flown, and we have no idea where to,' he said.

Angel nodded. 'Let's go home.'

* * *

It was still dark, but thankfully the moon was shining when Angel put the car in the garage. All the lights in the bungalow were out — Mary must be asleep.

Although he was tired, he went up the garden to the shed and took out a spade. He selected a place in the flowerbed to dig a small hole only six centimetres deep. Then he took out the Beretta and put it in the green plastic bag he had taken from the wheelie bin. The M & S bag was quite large, so he had to fold it over and round the gun several times to make the package as small as possible. Then he dropped it into the hole and covered it with earth.

SIX

Angel woke up. He put his hand out to touch Mary but she wasn't there. He opened his eyes. The room was in semi-darkness. The bedroom curtains were closed. He turned his head and squinted at the clock on the bedside table.

Ten o'clock! He should have been at the station. Why hadn't Mary woken him up? Then he realised it was Saturday. He sighed with relief. He sat up, swivelled his legs out of bed, pushed on his slippers and put on his dressing gown. He went to the window and pulled back one of the curtains. The sun was high and brilliant in a clear blue sky.

He ambled out of the bedroom along the hall to the kitchen. The door was open. Mary had her back to him; she was at the kitchen sink washing up a frying pan with uncharacteristic violence.

'Good morning, sweetheart,' he said as his hands went under her arms and his lips to her neck.

'Good morning,' she said stiffly. 'And what time did you get in last night?'

Angel realised he was in trouble. He pulled away from her. 'Can I smell scrambled eggs?' he asked wistfully. Mary's scrambled eggs were usually much better than his attempts, and she knew it.

'The canteen is closed,' she said. 'What time did you get in last night?'

'Erm about . . . about midnight.'

'Pardon?'

'About one o'clock.'

'Try again.'

Angel sniffed. 'Look, Mary,' he said. 'If you know, why do you ask?'

'It was half past four.'

'Was it really? I thought you were asleep.'

'I was. Until you slammed the door shut. Whatever were you doing out at that hour? I messaged you to ask where you were — why didn't you reply?'

He checked his phone. She was right — two missed messages. 'I'm so sorry, love, I had my phone on silent. We had to be quiet — we were trying to arrest two villains, but we had to find them first.'

'Did you catch them?'

'Nearly.'

'Nearly means you didn't. What a waste of time.'

Angel thought for a moment. 'Have we got last week's issue of the *Bromersley Chronicle*?'

Mary frowned. 'What for? We've got *this* week's. It only came yesterday. Who wants a week-old paper? I *might* have thrown it out. Look in the paper rack.'

He thought she probably had thrown it out. She was always throwing things out. Over the years, she had thrown away many a thing that he had wanted to keep.

'Will do,' he said. 'I'm going for a quick shower. I'll be about twenty minutes.'

She didn't say anything.

When Angel returned to the kitchen later, spotlessly clean and in a sports jacket and grey trousers, he found that Mary had made a pot of coffee for both of them, and had cooked him some scrambled eggs on toast. Also on the table was a copy of the *Bromersley Chronicle*. He snatched it up eagerly to check the date. It *was* 11 November.

He grinned at her. She smiled back.

'Thank you, darling. You're a marvel,' he said, and then he dashed across the kitchen and enfolded her in his arms.

'I worry about you,' Mary said, returning his embrace. 'I get frightened when you're out all night mixing with murderers, thieves, rogues and whatever. I worry in case you won't come back.'

'Well, don't. I will always come back to you, darling. I never take silly chances.'

They stayed in each other's arms for a few moments, then she forced a smile and said, 'Will you do me a favour?'

Angel frowned. He was on dangerous ground. Whatever he said he could be in trouble. He took a risk. 'Of course,' he said, not showing his wariness.

'Will you take me to Cheapo's? I don't like driving through the town on a Saturday. It's so busy.'

He smiled. 'Of course I will.'

'Your breakfast's getting cold.'

'Yes,' he said. 'But there's something else I must do first.'

He ran back to their bedroom to collect the newspaper with the hole in the small ads page. He put the two together. The piece cut out from the small ads section read:

Self-Catering Accommodation

Apartment in beautiful countryside. En-suite. Twin beds. Complete with modern gas oven, fridge, TV, shower, etc. Recently re-carpeted throughout. No pets. No children. Suit couple. Reasonable rates. Phone: Bromersley 876661.

Angel returned to the kitchen . . . to Mary, his breakfast and his thoughts.

* * *

After breakfast, Angel went into the sitting room. He sat down, took out his mobile and tapped in a number. It was soon answered. It was a girl's voice.

'The Bull Hotel.'

'I'm phoning about the advertisement in the paper about the self-catering accommodation . . .'

'Sorry, it's taken for the moment.'

Angel had to be quick.

'If we couldn't get in before Christmas, I was thinking about two weeks in February,' he said.

'Well, I can't say for sure if it will be free. You see, it was let to two gentlemen this morning, and they said they might want it for a month or longer.'

Angel's heart leapt.

The girl continued. 'If you're still interested I should enquire in a month.'

'I will. Could you give me the address?'

'It's simply the Bull Inn, Cropstitch, Bromersley.'

'One more thing . . . does it have its own entrance?'

'Yes. Up some steps outside. And the door is on the first floor.'

'That sounds good. Thank you. Goodbye.'

Angel was delighted. Cropstitch was only three miles out of town. He had an idea.

He went into the bedroom, where Mary had just changed her dress and shoes and was brushing her hair.

'Did you want to go to Cheapo's now, sweetheart?'

'If that's convenient to you?'

'Yes. I'll get the car out.'

Ten minutes later, as Angel stopped the car at the entrance of the supermarket, he said, 'I've a little job in Cropstitch I can see to while you're in there.'

Mary's eyes flashed. She was not pleased. 'I don't do the weekly shop for entertainment, Michael. There are plenty of things I'd rather be doing.'

He gave her a big smile. 'Won't take me long. I'll be back before you're halfway round the store. Bye, love.' Then he let in the clutch and sailed away.

* * *

Mary watched her husband drive slowly down the car park lane.

She bit her lip. It drove her wild that he left all the boring jobs to her. Surely most grown men could manage the occasional shopping trip without making up a 'job' they had to do to get out of it? And then there was his actual job, which kept him out till all hours doing who knew what. She wanted him to have a safer, less demanding career where his life was not constantly in danger. Despite all his faults, she was still passionately in love with him, but if he kept on leaving all the drudgery to her, she knew that would change.

As he went out of sight in a muddle of cars at the end of the lane, Mary shrugged and tightened her grip on her shopping bag, and made her way through the automatic glass doors into the store.

* * *

Angel drove through the centre of Bromersley and along Wakefield Road for about two miles past the rhubarb sheds to a narrow lane signposted to Cropstitch. He passed a few old houses, a small church, a tiny post office and a pub, the Bull. There were no pedestrians. There were a few cars parked outside the houses and several on the main street. He couldn't see Brown's car anywhere. There was a gravel car park in front of the Bull but there were no cars on it.

Angel parked his car outside the church and walked back to the Bull.

His feet crunched over the gravel on the forecourt of the pub. His eyes took in the layout of the place.

At the front of the building, a freshly painted black-and-white wooden staircase rose round a corner to a balcony and a door one storey up, most certainly the entrance to the flat.

He reached the main entrance to the Bull on the ground floor. He opened the door, and a bell tinkled above his head as he stepped down into the low-roofed old bar room.

The owner had retained all the 'olde worlde' features. Even so, there were no customers.

Angel climbed on to a bar stool and glanced around the room. It was not very big. Four tables with three or four chairs per table. There was an old-fashioned fireplace with newspaper and sticks showing through the bars of the grate, ready to be lit when needed. There were a couple of doors just behind where he was sitting, leading to the toilets and probably to another bar.

A smartly dressed man wearing an apron came through a door behind the far end of the bar. He was polishing a glass with a tea towel.

'Good afternoon, sir,' he said. 'What can I get you?'

'Good afternoon. Half a bitter, please. Where is everybody?'

'It's the match. Bromersley's playing away. But we're never very busy on a Saturday afternoon. The village is dead.'

The man delivered the glass of beer on a coaster.

Angel gave him a ten-pound note.

The man put it in the till, took out some coins, then turned back and passed over the change.

'Thank you, sir,' the man said, then went back the way he came. 'Ring the bell on the bar if you want anything.'

Angel looked at his watch. He had plenty of time. He could finish his beer, maybe have another nose round the village. He wasn't looking for trouble, but he did want to know for certain that Brown and Smith were housed in the pub. Knowing them both to be armed, he would have to summon the specialist armed unit from Wakefield to assist him in arresting them. That would be easy. Dangerous, but easy. Then he would chase up the lab results on the priest's murder and get on with that. He looked at his watch. He must drink up and get back to collect Mary.

Suddenly, he felt a hard tap on his shoulder and turned to see who it was.

Then it was if all hell was let loose: he met a man's closed fist with his mouth.

'I'll teach you to keep frigging following me!' the man screamed.

Angel fell back with the impact. He pulled away from the bar, stood up and turned to face his assailant.

It was Ezra Brown.

Brown threw another punch. Angel dodged back tidily, and again as Brown swiped a third time.

Angel blew out a metre of air. He was furious. Amid the shower of blows, Angel managed to grab Brown by the lapels of his jacket. He gave him a good shake.

'I want you in jail or off my patch, Brown,' he said icily. 'There's no place for you in a civilised society.'

Then Angel gave him a powerful, teeth-rattling upper-cut with his right, then another, then another, until Brown wasn't fully aware what was going on.

Angel pushed him away.

Brown staggered backwards, straightened up, shook his head to clear it and came back at Angel with a heavy blow directed at the stomach. Angel bent forward to minimise the impact and delivered two heavy punches at Brown's sides, one from each hand from the bent position.

While Brown was recovering, Angel grabbed his right arm and pulled it up his back until he hollered with pain.

'You frigging bastard!' Brown screamed. 'My arm! My arm!' He lunged out with a clenched fist at Angel. Every time he attempted it, Angel edged his arm up a little further.

'All right!' he yelled. 'All right!'

Angel would have to frog-march Brown to his car outside the church. It was a long way to take a man with his arm up his back.

Angel opened the pub door. He forced Brown up the step. They were crossing the gravel when a car came from round the corner. It drove straight on to the gravel and across their path. Angel saw the registration number of the car: AHE 156. The driver was Smith.

He would have to think quickly. Perhaps he shouldn't have been so quick to bury the Beretta.

He immediately pulled Brown's right arm a centimetre higher.

'My arm!' Brown shrieked, hutching up as far as he could.

His jacket opened slightly and Angel saw the butt of a gun surrounded by light-brown leather. Angel pulled the gun from Brown's shoulder holster, releasing his grip on the man's arm. 'Look what I've found.'

Brown blew out a length of fresh air, exercised his shoulder and said, 'What you going to do with that?'

'Put your hands up and stand over there,' Angel said.

They were two metres apart.

Smith opened the car door and crouched behind it. 'Mr Policeman, if you don't release him, I have a Smith & Wesson here that has eight rounds in it. I'll spend all eight rounds in you.'

Smith then bobbed his head down behind the door and waved the gun at him.

'You do know a car door doesn't stop bullets, don't you, Mr Smith?' Angel replied.

'Oh, Reg,' Brown whined, 'do whatever he says.'

'Very wise,' Angel said. 'First, come from behind that door. Stand there where I can see you, with your hands in the air . . . and throw your gun towards me.'

'Don't be daft, Angel,' Smith said. 'I'm not doing that. You must think I fell out of a tree.'

Angel's muscles tightened. He pressed the gun into Brown's temple and said, 'All right. Say goodbye to your boss, Reg.'

A tear rolled down Brown's cheek. 'For God's sake, do as he says, Reg.'

'I'll give you three seconds, Reg,' Angel said.

Brown yelled, '*Reg! Do as he says!*'

Angel began counting. 'One . . . two . . .'

The gun landed on the gravel by Angel's feet.

Smith closed the door and stood in the middle of the small car park.

'That's better,' Angel said.

Brown sighed.

Behind Angel, the small man with a beard and long hair came out of the flat. He silently moved along the balcony until he was above and directly behind Angel. In his hand was a gun. He looked down at his target, then tightened his top lip back against his teeth. He stood with his feet apart, and holding the gun with both hands, aimed at Angel's back.

Both Brown and Smith tried to avoid showing that they had seen him, but were poised and ready to spring into action.

Angel bent down to pick up Smith's gun just as the man pulled the trigger.

There was a loud report.

Hot lead hit the gravel.

Angel spontaneously whipped round and looked up in the direction of the source as Brown and Smith pounced on him.

Brown got him down on his back while gripping the wrist holding the Walther. Smith went straight for his gun, the Smith & Wesson in Angel's other hand.

In the struggle, the Walther went off.

A gunshot ricocheted round the car park.

It was all over in seconds.

Smith pointed the gun at Angel. 'Keep still. If you don't keep still, I'll shoot your frigging arm off. Lie on your stomach. Put your hands on your head.'

Brown was all smiles. 'You coppers think you're so smart, don't you?' he said, pointing his gun at him.

Angel didn't reply.

Brown called up to the balcony. 'Well done, Moss. Now quickly pack the bags and put them back in the car.'

The hairy Moss smiled, flashing his teeth, waved his acknowledgement and ran along the balcony and through the door into the flat.

Smith put his gun back in his shoulder holster, turned to Brown and said, 'Shall I go up and help him?'

Brown nodded and said, 'Yes, and hurry.' Then he pointed his gun at Angel, lying face down in the middle of the car park, and added, 'I'll watch him.'

Smith rushed off to the stairs.

Several minutes later Moss came down the stairs carrying three suitcases. He was followed by Smith, carrying one. They put the luggage in the boot and then got into the car.

Brown, gun in hand and eyes locked on Angel, followed them.

Angel heard the car engine start. Gravel crunched under the tyres of the big car as it began to move.

From his prostrate position, Angel looked up tentatively, in case any one of the three lost their cool and shot him on the way out.

Moss reversed the car out of the Bull's car park on to the road with Smith and Brown still pointing their guns through the open car windows. They drove off at speed.

Angel stood up, brushing off his trousers and jacket. He pushed his hand through his hair and gave thanks that he was still alive.

What should he do next?

He put a call in to the station to report his sighting of the wanted car, and to add that a shot had been fired.

He looked at his watch.

Then he remembered: Mary!

SEVEN

Mary had been waiting for thirty-two minutes when Angel pulled up outside Cheapo's.

She was furious. At first she couldn't speak, she was that angry. But when she did get started, it was a torrent.

He had apologised profusely on arrival but he couldn't defend himself by telling her the truth. If he had mentioned anything about firearms she would have gone bananas and insisted that he resign from the police on the spot.

Angel put the two bags of shopping into the boot. Then they both got in the car and Angel drove them home.

Mary continued the barrage until Angel said, 'When you meet up with some people, it's not always easy to break away from them.'

'Who were these people? Were they so important that you couldn't tell them your wife was expecting you? That she would be standing outside a shop on a cold October day for half an hour?'

'Look, Mary,' he said, 'I was late, I couldn't help it, I have apologised, can't we drop it?'

The remainder of the journey was made in hostile silence.

Angel was thinking . . . He should get Don Taylor to see if he could get any of the villains' fingerprints from the flat at the Bull.

* * *

It was 8.30 a.m. on Monday, 21 November.

It was the day that Mr Levi was expecting Brown or Smith or both to call at his antiques shop to collect the extortionate payment for so-called insurance.

Mr and Mrs Levi were in the shop with DI Angel, DS Flora Carter and DC Scrivens.

Mrs Levi gripped her husband's upper arm tightly with both hands. Mr Levi's hand was shaking.

'Inspector Angel?'

'Yes, Mr Levi?'

In a small voice, Levi said, 'Do you still think this is a good idea, Inspector? I have the four hundred pounds in the till. I drew it out of the bank especially . . . I'm thinking of the consequences that might follow . . . if anything goes wrong.'

'I understand the difficulty you face, Mr Levi. But there isn't another way. This extortion has to stop. You cannot keep paying them for ever, can you?'

'Well . . . no. No, we can't.' He looked at his wife. She nodded and looked down.

'Try not to worry. There are three of us here today. There are thirty-odd officers at Bromersley Police Station, and three thousand more, some armed, we can call on in an emergency.'

Angel looked at his watch.

'What time does the shop open?'

'Nine o'clock.'

'We shall have to conceal ourselves.'

It wasn't a big shop, but Angel spotted a beautifully decorated antique Japanese three-part screen, which was folded and standing against the wall. He reached out to it, opened it up and stood it across the corner of the room.

'Do you have a small stool or a sturdy box, Mr Levi?'

The shopkeeper turned to his wife, who said, 'I have a kitchen stool. I'll fetch it.'

She rushed off through the door behind the counter and returned in seconds carrying a sturdy-looking stool.

Angel smiled. 'Thank you. Just the thing.'

He put it behind the screen, sat down and pulled the third part of the screen slightly towards himself so that he couldn't be seen from any part of the shop. He came out from behind the screen.

'That's me set up. Flora, when the mark comes in, could you pretend to be a customer who can't make up her mind about which vase to buy? Better put two vases on the counter. And Mr Levi, would you do the best you can to persuade her to have one or the other? As you would normally do, I suppose. If the mark seems to be waiting for you to leave before he gets started, you can walk out of the shop and move away from the shopfront altogether. I'll call you back in if things kick off — if I don't, you'd better come back inside two minutes later. And bring some handcuffs.'

DS Carter smiled. 'Yes, sir. But I'm not good at acting.'

Mr Levi said, 'I'm no actor myself.'

Angel looked at him. 'Just pretend. It's only for a minute or two. Detective Carter has the most to say in this little drama, you know.'

Then Angel turned to Scrivens. 'I want you to park your car so that you're well away from the shop, but, at the same time, you can see everybody who comes through the shop door. You know what Brown and Smith look like. You've seen the photographs. If either or both of them approach the door, text me quickly. And you'll see when DS Carter comes out. Join her coming back into the shop and bring some handcuffs.'

'Right, sir.'

'Any questions?'

Mrs Levi said, 'What can I do, Inspector?'

Angel smiled at her. 'You can be first reserve. Lock the back door. Stay in the house. And stop worrying.'

Angel looked at his watch. 'It's nine o'clock. Places everybody, please. Open the shop in your usual way, Mr Levi, please.'

Mrs Levi squeezed her husband's arm reassuringly and went out of the door behind the counter into the living part of the building.

Levi switched on the outside lights, unbolted the shop door, let DC Scrivens out, turned the open/closed sign round, then returned to his usual position behind the counter.

Carter came up to the counter on the opposite side.

Angel took to the stool behind the screen.

All was set.

It was ten o'clock before any customers came into the shop. Then it became very busy for two hours, with Mr Levi making numerous sales. At times, the doorbell hardly seemed to stop ringing.

On such occasions, Carter stood back from the counter saying, 'I'm in no hurry. I just can't make my mind up.'

Angel stayed hidden behind the screen.

Scrivens had found a suitable place to park his unmarked car so he could observe the antiques shop door.

The shop was suddenly quiet.

The phone rang. It was on the counter.

Levi reached out for it. 'Levi's Antiques,' he said.

Carter pulled away from the counter to give Levi some privacy.

'Look, son,' the unmistakable voice of Ezra Brown said, 'do you think I'm stupid enough to walk into your shop and conduct business with you while you've got coppers there waiting to play peek-a-boo?'

Levi's hand began to shake. His heart raced. It nearly exploded.

'Well, *do you?*' Brown bawled.

'Er . . . erm . . . no,' Levi whispered.

'Your premium's now gone up to *five* hundred pounds a month,' Brown said. 'And don't try and betray me again or you and your wife will be seeing the biggest bonfire you've ever seen. And it will start just where you're standing. Have you got that?'

Levi swallowed. 'Yes.'

'Now pack the five hundred in an envelope and keep it on you until I tell you different. Right?'

'Yes.'

'And get rid of those coppers.'

The line went dead.

Levi slowly replaced the phone. His face was as white as lilies on a grave.

Angel came from behind the screen massaging his lower back. He was numb through sitting on the stool for so long. He looked at Levi, pointed to the phone. 'That sounded important.'

Levi bit his lip. 'It was Brown. He knows you're here. He says he won't come while there are any police about.'

Angel's face was screwed up in thought. 'Are you sure he didn't say anything else?'

'Yes.'

Carter said, 'I don't think he'll leave it for long.'

Angel nodded in agreement.

Then he turned back to Levi. 'You'll let me know the minute he contacts you, won't you?'

'Oh yes,' Levi said.

* * *

Angel slumped down in the swivel chair in his office and turned to DS Carter, who had followed him in.

'What a waste of a morning,' he said.

'How did Brown find out that we were in there waiting for him?' Carter said.

'I shouldn't have posted Ted outside. Maybe they recognised him or knew the car from somewhere. It wasn't his fault. I was entirely to blame. Also, I don't altogether trust Mr Levi, Flora. He's very afraid. His wife is even worse. Even at the last push, he had the four hundred ready in the till in case I could be persuaded to change my mind and agree to go ahead with the payoff.'

Their mobiles both began to ring at the same time.

They exchanged puzzled glances and proceeded to answer them.

Angel opened his first. 'Yes?' he said.

A voice seemingly coming through a loudspeaker said, 'This is a recorded emergency call from the Convent of the Holy Reliquary of the Finger of Saint Ethel. Bandits on the premises. Please attend urgently. This is a recorded emergency—'

It was Angel's own voice.

* * *

When Angel arrived at the convent, the big doors were closed. He stopped his car at the side of the road, aware that Carter and Scrivens were parking behind him, and ran to the door at the side. It was not locked. He pressed the sneck and pushed open the door into the garden. Then he ran across the short drive to the front door of the convent.

He tried the door. It was unlocked. He pushed it open. He remembered that the Reverend Mother's office and the sitting room were on the first floor. He ran past the pictures Brown and Smith had attacked on their last visit and up the stairs. At the top he stopped and listened.

He could hear somebody talking. It seemed to be coming from the sitting room. Angel turned to Carter and Scrivens, who were coming up the stairs behind him, and put his finger to his lips.

The speaker sounded like a man. 'I'm not leaving until you find me the money. It's a very good investment, seeing how your beautiful things break so easily . . .'

'It's Brown,' Angel whispered. 'I'll go in and leave the door ajar. You two listen in.'

They both nodded.

Angel opened the door and walked in. Everybody turned to look at him. He wasn't pleased to see Brown holding a gun.

Brown had the Walther trained on the Reverend Mother, but when he saw Angel he turned the barrel on the detective.

All five nuns were standing in a bunch to one side of the fireplace, with the intruders on the other side, rather like a hastily arranged family photograph. The hearth was littered with broken china and glass. Smith was standing like a statue; with his arm out in front of him, between finger and thumb, he held a figurine of the Virgin and Child. He lowered his arm when he saw Angel.

Angel said, 'What's all this?'

Brown's eyes flashed with anger. 'Put your hands up, policeman. What are you doing here? Always following me around?'

Angel put up his hands. 'Haven't you realised that these women aren't like you? They don't worship money. They've taken a vow of poverty. They've barely enough to live on. And all you can do is deliberately damage everything of theirs you touch. You're wasting your time here, Brown. They shouldn't be on your sucker list.'

'Shut your mouth!'

'Certainly,' Angel said. 'But I think it's only fair to tell you that the place is surrounded. You might as well give me that gun and give yourselves up.'

He was not very hopeful that Brown would really believe him and surrender the gun.

Smith's eyebrows shot up. He put the ornament down on a nearby side table, took out his gun and looked at Brown.

Brown made straight for the door. Smith followed.

Angel lowered his hands.

They dashed out of the room on to the landing.

Angel saw them race down the stairs.

Carter and Scrivens appeared. They had been hiding in the next room with the door ajar.

'Follow them, Ted, at a very safe distance. I don't think they know you. But be careful. Remember they're both armed. I want to find out where they're living, or what other poor soul is being milked by them. See where they go. *Don't approach them.*'

'Right, sir,' he said, and rushed off.

Then Angel turned to Carter. 'You might as well return to the office, Flora. The lab results on the death of that priest are due.'

'I'll see if I can chase them up, sir,' she said, and went out.

The sisters crowded round Angel all smiles and all speaking at once. The Reverend Mother put up a hand and they went silent.

Sister Teresa put up a finger as a request to speak.

'Yes, Teresa? Did you want to say something?'

'I wanted on behalf of us all to thank the inspector for that timely intervention,' she said.

The sisters murmured their agreement.

Angel smiled.

The Reverend Mother unfastened the top button of her scapular and pulled out the small red plastic medallion on a cord round her neck. 'It was in answer to this amazing little alarm button.'

Sister Precious pulled an indignant face. 'It was in answer to our *prayers.*'

The Reverend Mother and Precious exchanged glares.

'I expect it was in answer to both,' Angel said.

Sister Clare said, 'Inspector, are there many police surrounding the house?'

'And have they all got guns, Inspector?' Emma asked.

'No guns,' Angel said. 'I'm afraid the house is not surrounded and there are no more than the three of us. Little white lies of mine, I confess.'

'Well, it chased them away nicely,' the Reverend Mother said. 'Let's hope your speech about our vow of poverty will keep them away for good.'

Angel's eyes betrayed his slight embarrassment. 'Sorry, Reverend Mother.'

'Please be assured it wasn't a criticism, Inspector. What you said was true. And I wish people outside the Church understood that. Although the Church owns a lot of property, it is still short of working capital to keep it going.'

Angel nodded. 'I must be off. Keep the alarm button with you for another week or so until we're sure you're safe.'

'I will. Thank you, Inspector,' the Reverend Mother said, 'for everything.'

Then she turned to the sisters. 'Let us all now retire to the chapel to give thanks.'

* * *

Ted Scrivens was off to a bad start, because when he reached the convent front door, he saw Brown and Smith running towards the back gate, presumably to their car. Unfortunately, Scrivens's car was parked outside the front gate, on the other side of the convent grounds. He would have to move fast to catch up with them.

He didn't waste a moment, and while travelling towards the back gate, he was stopped at a crossroads by traffic lights and saw the big car pass in front of him, heading down the main Sheffield Road toward the town centre.

When the lights changed he took a right and followed in their tracks. Soon he caught them up at a roundabout, bunched in by a group of other cars.

Soon the traffic was flowing freely again. Brown's car went up a side road, Cavendish Street, where many Bromersley solicitors and accountants had offices. Scrivens followed. Brown stopped at a roadside parking spot in a bank of six.

Scrivens had to continue. He passed them, went to the top of the street and, looking for a parking place, took four right turns to bring him driving up Cavendish Street again, still looking for a place to park.

At the top of the road, he turned right and pulled up in front of some offices, and put a card on the windscreen that said, 'Police on Duty'. Then he locked the car and rushed back towards Brown's car.

And then, *disaster*!

He saw Brown and Smith on foot coming towards him. They were looking at each other and talking.

Scrivens looked immediately to his right. There was a door. On the wall next to it were several brass plates, one under the other. He didn't read any of them. He went straight through the door into a hall with a staircase facing him. He ran up the stairs and through the first office door. It led to a reception desk. A young lady popped up from behind a computer and said, 'Can I help you, sir?'

The office was at the front of the building.

Scrivens went to the window and looked down at the pavement. He saw the two men still conversing with each other. He sighed and made for the door.

The young lady repeated, 'Can I help you, sir?'

'Erm. No. Excuse me. And thank you,' Scrivens said, and he rushed out of the office, down the stairs and back on to the pavement. He ran a while until he saw them. Then he crossed the road to make his observation of them less obvious.

They were entering the shopping centre, so he closed the gap between them. He was a little surprised when he saw the two enter the Golden Dragon, a Chinese restaurant.

It had a flashing neon sign incorporated into a large painting of a dragon across the front of the restaurant. From the pavement, through the large windows, he could see several customers inside sitting at some of the twenty or so tables set out with spotlessly white cloths, shiny cutlery and tidy condiment sets.

Scrivens ambled past the door of the restaurant and made his way up the street for about a hundred metres. He found that if he turned a little way along a side road and positioned himself opposite a low wall, he could see the door of the restaurant over the wall without being seen from there himself.

He leaned back against the wall and yawned. This was the boring part of the job. Over the eight years he had been in the force he had spent half of it following suspects and waiting for them to make a move.

However, on this occasion he didn't have long to wait.

About fifteen minutes later, Brown and Smith came out through the doors and made their way in the direction of their car.

Scrivens followed carefully. When he saw them opening their car doors, he quickly went to fetch his own car. But when he drove back, they had gone.

He drove down Cavendish Street, but when he was at the bottom he didn't know which way to go. He turned right and mooned around there hoping to pick them up, but he had lost them.

He parked the car, returned to the Golden Dragon restaurant, and ordered a pot of tea with lemon, and sweet-and-sour pork with fried rice.

He didn't ask any questions, but he used his other senses. He smelled burning as soon as he entered the restaurant, and he saw grey and black scorch marks on the white wall over the 'in' and 'out' serving doors between the dining area and the kitchen.

He paid his bill and returned to Bromersley Police Station.

EIGHT

The telephone rang in Levi's Antiques. Mr Levi took the call.

'Have you got that five hundred pounds in used notes wrapped up in a packet?' Brown said.

Levi's blood ran cold. He cleared his throat. 'Yes.'

'Have you got it on you?'

Levi put his shaking hand under the till for it. 'Yes.'

'Speak to nobody. Just take it — with your mobile — and walk quickly to the Northern Bank on King Street and wait outside. Someone will contact you. You have four minutes.'

The line went dead.

Levi hesitated. Then he replaced the phone, pushed the packet into his inside pocket and dashed out of the shop without speaking to anybody.

He almost ran to King Street but didn't want to draw any attention to himself. He looked around him and wondered who might be watching him. He saw no faces or cars he knew. Just as he arrived at the bank, a little out of breath, his mobile rang.

'You only just made it, I see,' Brown said. 'Now, go to the main door of the town hall and stand on the top step. You'll be contacted there. You have two and a half minutes.'

Levi looked around but could not see Brown, his car nor any familiar faces, but he knew somebody must be watching.

He duly arrived at the top step outside the town hall as his mobile began to ring.

'Right, now,' Brown said, 'take the zebra crossing and make your way down Fleet Street to the post office. Wait outside on the pavement. You'll be contacted there. That'll take no more than forty seconds.'

Levi arrived outside the post office inside the forty seconds. He was perspiring. He wiped his forehead with his handkerchief and looked around. There was nobody around that he knew. A few people came in and out of the doors behind him. There were no parking places on the narrow street and there was very little road traffic.

His mobile rang again.

'Right, Levi, now come to the edge of the pavement, take the packet out of your pocket and give it to me.'

Levi looked up and saw Brown's car approaching him and slowing down, the driver's window wound down. The car pulled up close to Levi, and Brown held out a hand for the packet.

Levi passed it to him.

With the car still on the move, Brown said, 'It'll be five hundred next month, Levi. And it'll go up more if you don't get rid of that copper.'

Then Brown put his foot down on the accelerator and whizzed down the street into the busy traffic junction at the bottom.

* * *

Angel closed the office door, put his hat on the hanger on the side of the stationery cupboard and sat down in the swivel chair. He looked at Carter and pointed to a chair at the other side of the desk. 'Flora, I'm getting to the end of my tether with Brown. I can't move him out of the area, nor can I arrest him. We'll never be able to arrest him as long as he and his sidekicks have guns. And the super won't permit me to withdraw a handgun from the armoury.'

'Why?' Carter said.

Angel shrugged. 'Because he's the boss,' he said. 'My firearms licence is valid and I've attended all the refresher courses.'

Carter said, 'Is it because possessing guns may incur all sorts of risks and possible casualties?'

'Well, yes. *And* because it could involve him in a lot of paperwork.'

'What do we do then, sir?'

'If we could only find out where they hang out, where they relax . . . That's why I've sent Ted Scrivens out to follow them.'

'Then we could call in the specialist armed unit from Wakefield.'

'There's more than one way to skin a cat.'

There was a knock at the door. It was DS Donald Taylor, head of the SOCO team.

'I've got the lab result on the samples taken from the murdered priest, Richard Morgan, sir,' he said.

Angel suddenly sat up. He looked refreshed. He rubbed his hands together in welcome expectation.

'Sit down and translate them for us, Don,' he said.

'That's easy.' Taylor shuffled through the pages of the report. 'Here's the bit you want. It says that there were particles of the person's own skin, specs of charcoal and traces of beeswax and resin found on the clothes.'

Angel frowned. 'I can understand the presence of his own skin. The wax could be from all the candles that are around, and the charcoal from the flames, but where does resin come in?'

'Perhaps he played the violin?' Taylor said. 'Don't you clean the strings with it or something?'

'I think resin *creates friction*,' Angel said, 'allowing the bow to grip the strings and make them vibrate more clearly. Anyway, if he was musical at all, I would visualise a man of six foot four playing double bass. Or maybe the resin was from the murderer and he or she is the musician.'

Taylor said, 'There's a bit more. We also discovered two hair specimens, including some root pulp — which means we can tell that the hair belonged to a woman with South Asian ancestry. Of course, I will leave this file with you.'

Angel said, 'We don't know anybody in this case from that part of the world, Flora, do we?'

'Well, I don't, sir,' she said.

Taylor's phone rang. 'I'm wanted, sir. If you will excuse me?'

'Yes. Thank you, Don.'

He rushed off.

Angel sat at his desk with pursed lips and his nose turned upward, a thoughtful pose.

'What's the matter, sir?' asked Carter.

Angel shook his head, hesitated, then said, 'I'm disappointed, Flora. I had expected more definitive information . . . about one particular member of the community . . . someone to look into that might have led to a conviction.'

Carter nodded.

There was a knock at the door. It was Scrivens.

Angel's eyebrows went up. 'Ah. Come in, lad. I was wondering where you had got to. Sit down. What have you found out?'

Scrivens made his report to them and finished up by asking Angel if he could claim the Chinese meal on his expenses.

'Well, did you enjoy it?'

'Oh *yes*, sir.'

Angel kept a straight face. 'You should have said "no" and I could have allowed it.'

Scrivens looked confused. 'Well, I did find out that the restaurant has probably become one of Brown's unfortunate clients. They'd had a kitchen fire that morning. I tried to ask about it, but they weren't giving much away.'

Angel stood up. 'That's good work, Ted,' he said. Then he turned to Carter. 'Come on, Flora. Let's get down to the Golden Dragon.'

She stood up. 'I'll get my stuff,' she said as she rushed off.

'Scrivens, we've had a bit of news about the forensics for the death of that priest. See if you can find out if Father Morgan played a musical instrument, or if any of the nuns at the convent play — a *stringed* musical instrument, mind. There were traces of resin on his body, and we're not sure where it came from.'

Scrivens nodded.

'And if you trip over anyone there who might be of South Asian descent, I want to know about it.'

* * *

The Chinese man in the white coat said, 'You don't want to eat?'

Angel took out his warrant card and showed it to the man. 'No, thank you. We're police and we want to see the owner, please.'

'Oh yes. Excuse me, please,' the man said. He went off.

Angel saw the grey and black scorch marks on the wall and ceiling above the serving doors. He nudged Carter and pointed up to them.

She looked up, saw them and nodded.

The man in the white coat returned. 'Please follow me.'

He showed Angel and Carter into an office.

There was a very well-dressed man seated at a large desk.

He stood up. 'Please come in. Sit down. My name is Lo. I am the proprietor of this restaurant. What can I do for the police?'

'This is Sergeant Carter and I am Inspector Angel of the Bromersley police force. Mr Lo, we're looking for an armed gang who are calling on businesses; they are purporting to be in the insurance business. They scare and bully owners into paying exorbitant insurance premiums for unnecessary so-called cover. I have reason to believe that they visited you earlier today. Is that correct?'

Mr Lo lowered his chin on to his chest thoughtfully then looked up.

'Inspector Angel,' Lo said, 'am I legally bound to tell you the truth?'

Angel blinked and frowned. 'Well, yes, Mr Lo. You are. If you told me an untruth it would be seen as obstructing the police in the execution of their duty . . . you would be breaking the law.'

'Then I decline to answer the question. May I put a hypothetical question to you, Inspector?'

'Of course.'

Mr Lo thought a moment and then said, 'If I had a happy, healthy wife and two children, and a successful business, and was approached by someone who needed to sponge a relatively small amount out of me every month or they might seriously harm my family, burn down my restaurant, poison my customers and so on, what should I do?'

'Tell me all you can about that someone and his gang and assist me in having them all arrested,' Angel said. 'Because if you don't, the months will change to years and the payments will go up and up until you can't afford them. Then you will *have* to do something. Your attitude will harden and you will try to do something on your own. The gang will retaliate, assault your family, burn down your restaurant and continue to milk you until you have nothing. There is no limit to what this gang will do now that they realise how easy it is to frighten people.'

Lo let out a long breath. His lips trembled.

'We have quite a file on this little gang, Mr Lo,' Angel said. 'What we don't know is where they live or where they're staying. Lately, they've always been on the move. As soon as we learn where they are, they've moved on to somewhere else. We only need forty minutes' notice and we could have the place surrounded by armed officers, trained for the very purpose of dealing with armed criminals.'

'All right, Inspector, you've made a sound case for cooperating with the police. What do you want me to do?'

Angel exchanged glances with Carter.

Then Angel said, 'Did you give them any money?'

'No,' Lo said. 'He took it. I said that most customers pay by card and that I would have to go to the bank and withdraw it. He didn't believe me. He was very angry. He raided the till in the restaurant. I don't yet know exactly how much he took, but he said he would be back for the balance in a few days.'

Angel thought for a moment and then said, 'Are you prepared to assist the police in putting this gang in prison?'

'Yes, provided that my wife and my two daughters and my staff are completely out of danger.'

'Can you send your wife and your girls away somewhere . . . with a friend or relative for a week or so?'

Lo half closed his eyes in thought. 'My mother has been eager to see more of them. She lives in Birmingham, and I think she would be happy to have them for a short while . . . I think that could be easily arranged.'

'Good. Now here's what we'll do . . .'

* * *

It had been a long day and Angel was tired when he returned home.

He had steak and kidney pie, one of his favourites, for dinner. When he had finished his second helping, he turned to Mary and said, 'That was delicious, darling. What time is your train on Wednesday? I shall miss you. Did I say I'll take you to the station?'

Mary looked at her husband. 'Are you talking about Miriam?'

He sniffed. 'Your beloved sister,' he said. 'Of course.'

'Can't you come with me?'

'I'm neck deep in this murder case. Although I'll miss you, sweetheart, it would be selfish of me not to let you go. If you want to.'

Mary's face brightened. 'You know I want to go. I'll worry about you on your own. But I'll leave you stacks of meals in the fridge, and the instructions with them.'

'Don't go to any trouble, love. I can go to the chippy and the pub. And I can knock up an omelette or two.'

'I'd better ring her to expect me,' she said, jumping up from the table.

Angel said, 'Don't stay on talking for ever. Two hours is long enough!'

Mary smiled. 'Don't be so sarcastic,' she called back from the hall.

Angel pursed his lips, breathed out long stream of air and went into the sitting room.

* * *

It was 11.45 p.m. on Monday 21 November. There had been a flurry of snow with a strong wind that day at teatime. It had stopped snowing, but now it was very cold and the wind was getting stronger and louder.

The landing on the first floor of the convent was in darkness. At the top of the stairs was a large stained-glass window depicting Jesus ascending into heaven. The window rattled and outside the wind howled, gusting round the convent and the chapel.

A shapeless figure tiptoed along the cold, black, draughty landing, then stopped at a door and flashed a torch up to the wording neatly painted on it: 'St Thomas'.

The rooms in the convent all had saints' names instead of numbers.

Turning the knob, the figure entered the room, closed the door, approached the bed, stopped and listened. Above the wind could be heard the steady breathing of the sister asleep in bed.

The intruder pulled a stiletto out of a shoulder holster and, after momentarily flashing the torch at their target, plunged the dagger into the sleeper's heart. A firm hand over the victim's mouth prevented any noise from escaping. A few seconds later, she was dead.

The shapeless figure withdrew the stiletto from the woman's heart, wiped it on the sheet and slipped it back into the holster. A moment's pause at the door to listen for the sounds of anything human, then it was gone.

NINE

It was Tuesday, 22 November.

The five o'clock morning bell rang out on the landing of the convent. This responsibility was arranged by rota, and this morning it was Sister Teresa's name on the roster. The bell was an instruction to the sisters to rise out of bed, wash, dress and read a set piece from the Bible in the privacy of their rooms.

By habit and tradition, the first who was ready would go into the kitchen and make a pot of tea for herself and her four sisters. That was usually the Reverend Mother. At this time of morning, the women were still observing the Great Silence — which began every evening immediately after Compline and lasted until after Lauds — so they would usually stand about in the kitchen in silence warming their hands on their cups and enjoying their drinks. They would then assemble in the chapel for the first service of the day, which consisted of psalms, scriptures and meditations.

When it became obvious that, very unusually, the Reverend Mother was not among the tea drinkers in the kitchen, Sister Precious put down her cup and shuffled out of the kitchen. She made for the stairs, which she had to take one at a time. She reached the door marked 'St Thomas' and knocked hard on it. She waited, knocked again, then turned the door knob and went into the little room.

The Reverend Mother was still in bed. When she saw her fixed staring eyes, her frozen grey face and the blood on the sheets, Sister Precious cried out, 'Lord, have mercy on us! Lord, have mercy!'

Then she went down on her knees by the bed.

The other nuns came running at the sound of her voice. On seeing the shape in the bed, the Reverend Mother's staring face and the blood, they too gasped and dropped to their knees. They were a little squashed together because the room was so small, but they joined Sister Precious praying silently, wiping away the occasional tear.

After a few minutes, Precious stood up, looked at the watch on her wrist and said, 'Sisters, a moment, if I may interrupt your prayers . . . and break the Great Silence again. In spite of this most tragic and evil event, I think we should keep our discipline. It will help us to stay strong, I am sure . . . We are three minutes late for Lauds. We should now retire to our chapel and say our prayers for the soul of the Reverend Mother, as well as the usual offices, resume the Great Silence and after Lauds inform Bishop Letterman and the police and deal with any other practical matters.'

Sister Clare stood up. 'Excuse me asking, Sister, but you're taking over the Reverend Mother's role a bit soon, aren't you?'

'Somebody has to be in charge, Sister Clare, and I was Reverend Mother here for more than twenty years before dear Julia . . . I have no wish to take up that burden again, and I would decline the responsibility if it were offered to me again. If you don't want to go to chapel for Lauds, I am not able to compel you. You must do what your conscience tells you.'

Then she turned away from her and looked at Sister Emma. 'What do you want to do, Sister Emma?'

'I am willing to go with everybody else,' Emma said, 'as long as we can pray together for the Reverend Mother's soul.'

'Yes, of course, we must do that, but do you think we should maintain our discipline and have Lauds now?'

'I suppose so.'

'And what do you want to do, Sister Teresa?'

'I agree with Emma.'

'You think we should maintain our discipline and have Lauds now?'

'Yes.'

Precious nodded with satisfaction. 'Right. In a few minutes, those who want to join in Lauds, make your way to the chapel.'

All the sisters attended.

* * *

It was ten minutes to nine when Angel and Carter arrived at the front door of the convent. It was opened by the diminutive elder nun.

Angel said, 'I was very sorry to hear the tragic news, Sister Precious.'

'Thank you, Inspector,' she said. 'The Lord giveth. The Lord taketh away. Come in.'

As they stepped through the door, they found two more nuns, Clare and Emma, standing in silence with heads bowed down.

Angel forced a smile and turned toward the nuns. 'I was sorry to hear about the very sad loss of your Reverend Mother. Our sincere condolences to you all.'

'Yes,' Carter said. 'She was a lovely lady.'

One of the nuns uttered a short, uncontrollable cry.

'If you will follow me,' Precious said.

She directed Angel and Carter up the stairs, along the landing to the Reverend Mother's room.

When Angel had seen the body, he ushered Sister Precious and Carter out on to the landing.

Then he took out his mobile and rang Detective Sergeant Taylor, the man in charge of the SOC team. 'Don, we have a woman murdered at the convent. It seems to be a similar MO to the murder of the priest.'

'Right, sir,' Taylor said. 'We'll be there in twenty minutes or so.'

Angel clenched his jaw. 'Make it fifteen minutes *on the button*,' he said, then he pushed the phone back into his pocket.

He turned to Precious. 'This room is a crime scene and as such is out of bounds. I want to interview you and the other three members of the community now, Sister. May we use your sitting room again?'

'Of course, Inspector. I'll go and inform them and meet you back there in a couple of minutes.'

She went off, muttering to herself as she shuffled away.

Angel turned to Carter. 'Flora, go round the ground-floor windows and both doors and all the locks. See if there's any sign of a break-in. Look in the outbuildings for any sign of a ladder. I want to know if anybody entered and left the convent overnight on the sly. Then join me in the sitting room.'

'Right, sir,' she said and rushed off.

Then he interviewed each of the nuns separately. All four knew of no reason why the Reverend Mother had been murdered. He discovered from each one that the front and back doors to the convent were locked most of the time during the day, and that they were certainly locked and bolted and the keys withdrawn each evening just before Compline, at about ten minutes past eight. The keys were then hung on the keyboard, which was on the inside of the metre cupboard under the stairs. All the sisters knew this and access to the keys was unrestricted.

During the interview with Sister Precious, she said, 'Inspector, I should like to point out that I have already phoned Bishop Letterman, who is spiritually and materially in charge of this convent, and told him that the Reverend Mother has been murdered. The Bishop has records on Father Morgan and the nuns which might be very useful to you. You will no doubt contact him.'

'I will indeed,' Angel said. 'And thank you for pointing that out to me.'

When the last of the four had gone out of the sitting room, Carter came into the room.

'Well Flora, what did you find?'

'I saw nothing to suggest that anybody had entered or left the building through a ground-floor window. The doors showed no signs of a break-in or of being forced. And I could not find a ladder anywhere.'

Angel wrinkled his nose and jutted out his chin grimly. 'That's what I feared,' he said. 'They all answered perfectly sensibly. They would make ideal witnesses. They knew exactly what to say, and yet one of them is guilty of the ghastly murder of two people.'

* * *

It was Wednesday morning, 23 November.

Angel drove the BMW into a parking space outside Bromersley station. He looked at his watch. 'What time does your train leave, love?'

'Eight thirteen, but it's from the platform over the bridge.'

'That's all right. Come on.'

'Michael, I don't like leaving you like this.'

Angel smiled. 'When you meet your Miriam, you'll start talking and you'll have that much to say — both of you — that you'll have forgotten all about me.'

They got out of the car, and he took her suitcase out of the boot. 'Got your ticket?'

'In my purse. There's a casserole for your dinner tonight in the oven. I've left a note on the oven top. Thirty minutes at number six.'

Angel made his way along the platform towards the steps to cross the bridge. Mary had to run beside him to keep up.

'What's the rush? You said there was plenty of time.'

He slowed down. 'Sorry, love. Now, you have a good time. Be careful down these steps.'

'Yes, thank you. You will look after yourself, won't you? Don't be doing anything dangerous. I don't want to leave you, Michael. I wish you were coming. It's not too late to change my mind.'

'You'll be all right once you meet up with Miriam. She's meeting you at Edinburgh Waverley, isn't she? Make sure you've got everything when you change at Leeds.'

'I will.'

He hefted her suitcase on to the train and put it on the baggage rack, then turned to her, took off his hat and gave her a big Hollywood kiss, which surprised and pleased her. He leapt off the train just as the doors were closing.

Mary had a shiver of excitement as the train pulled out and Angel was still on the platform waving to her.

Angel had a shiver of a very different kind . . .

* * *

As he was walking back to his car his mobile rang out.

He answered it.

A familiar voice said, 'This is a recorded emergency call from the Golden Dragon restaurant. Bandits on the premises. Bandits on the premises. Please attend urgently. This is a recorded emergency call—'

It was his own voice again. He pocketed the mobile.

His heart began to pound like the big drum in a Salvation Army Band.

He ran to his car.

He wasn't far from the restaurant, and was there in a few minutes.

Mr Lo was at the door and greeted him. 'You were very quick, Inspector. But they've been and gone. Brown and Smith came in waving their guns and demanding money. I said that I had very little cash here. They opened the till and helped themselves and were gone in a minute. I don't know how much they took. I will know later.'

Angel said, 'Which direction did they take?'

'They must have had their car parked somewhere near. They made their way into the busy market and were soon lost among the shoppers.'

'I'll see if I can find them. See you later, Mr Lo.'

'Good luck, Inspector.'

Angel returned to his car.

There could be as many as six police vehicles and two traffic wardens in the centre of Bromersley at that time searching for that car.

Angel drove away from the restaurant and turned left to search round the back of it and among car parks close by. The gang's car was not to be seen.

His mobile rang. It was a patrolman. 'Big black American car, licence number Alpha Hotel Echo 156 parked in front of the Feathers Hotel.'

Angel's eyes brightened.

'Well done, patrolman. And thank you.'

It took only two minutes to get to the Feathers Hotel. He could have been there a minute sooner if it had not been for traffic lights and dithering drivers.

He saw the car. It *was* the one. He gave a sigh of relief. Then he saw the little man who had shot at him, Moss, in the driving seat. That was a complication he hadn't expected. He sped past him and quickly turned left out of his eyeshot.

He hoped that Moss had not seen him, or if he had, that he thought Angel had not noticed him. He pulled up to the kerb and stopped. He needed thinking time.

He wanted to fix a magnetic GPS tracker to the gang's car so that he could monitor every move the gang made — a slap-and-track operation. He only needed a couple of seconds to drop it on to the underside of a wheel arch, but he needed to get Moss away from the car . . .

Just then, he spotted Detective Sergeant Taylor driving past in an unmarked car. Angel flashed his lights. Taylor saw him, stopped and ran across to Angel's car.

Angel lowered the window.

'Did you want me, sir?'

'Yes, Don. Get in a minute.'

Taylor ran round the car, opened the door and got in.

'Any good at acting, Don?'

'I dunno. Never done any.'

'Well, listen up.'

Five minutes later, Taylor walked down the street and round the corner to the front of the Feathers Hotel and the gang's car.

Angel followed him part of the way, managing to position himself among window shoppers so that he could see what was happening without being conspicuous.

Taylor approached the big black car and tapped on the driver's window.

The little man hesitated then lowered it five centimetres.

'Excuse me, is your name Moss?' he said.

The little man's eyebrows went up. He frowned, glanced behind and around and then looked back at Taylor. 'It might be, why?'

'There's a gentleman called Ezra Brown,' Taylor said. 'He told me your name . . . Mr Brown has had an accident . . . he urgently wants you to go to him. He's at the front of the Rocket Gymnasium, next to the Chinese restaurant.'

Taylor pointed. 'Just round the corner.'

Moss frowned again. 'Er, right.' He ran a hand jerkily through his mass of hair. 'Erm, what's happened?'

'I don't know. I was just passing. I don't know *him*. He asked me to find you and tell you. He wants your help. That's all I know.'

Taylor pulled away from the window and quickly made his way back to his own car to avoid any more questions from the hairy man.

Moss remained in the driver's seat rubbing his cheek. He rubbed his cheek for twenty or thirty seconds, then suddenly got out of the car and rushed away in the direction of the Rocket Gym.

When Moss was out of sight, Angel jumped up and made for the big car.

* * *

Back in his office, Angel watched his computer screen, eager to follow the movements of the gang's car. It was still outside the Feathers Hotel.

His landline phone rang, and he reached out for the handset.

It was the civilian receptionist. 'There's a Bishop Letterman here to see you, Inspector,' she said.

'Get somebody to show him to my office, please,' he said.

Bishop Letterman was a slim, soft-spoken man with greying hair. He wore a black suit with a purple front, a clerical collar and a black cape. He was carrying six light-brown paper files.

'Please sit down, Bishop. I am very pleased to meet you face to face. Have you brought me the records?'

'They're all here, as promised,' he said. 'I'm pleased to meet you, Inspector. Have you made any progress?'

Angel shook his head. 'I'm hoping that those records may give us a clue.'

'Are you saying you have no idea who the murderer is?'

'We have several suspects, Bishop.'

The Bishop thought a moment then said, 'I hope it is nobody in my flock. Do you believe that both murders were committed by the same person?'

'We have not reached any firm conclusions.'

Letterman nodded. 'If there's anything else I can help you with, Inspector . . .'

Angel rubbed his chin. 'There might be something, Bishop — some history or fact that is perhaps not in these files that might have some bearing on the murders. Is there anything like that? It might help us with our investigation.'

Letterman's eyebrows went up. 'How perceptive of you, Inspector. There is something. It concerns Sister Precious. The workings of the human mind are impossible to understand. About ten years after Sister Precious was admitted into the sisterhood — that's about forty years ago — a woman came to the convent and asked to see her, so I've been told. The woman said that she was Sister Precious's mother. Precious said she didn't know anything about the woman and that most certainly she was not her mother. The church engaged a private investigator, who confirmed that the woman's story was true. He also discovered that Precious's father had been hanged for murdering a woman he had lived with for several years.'

'So Sister Precious's father was a murderer.' Angel pursed his lips.

'But, Inspector,' the Bishop went on, 'I don't see how this can be relevant. Sister Precious is the epitome of what a Christian servant of God should be. That's why I said the workings of the human mind are impossible to comprehend. She is a little crusty and not easy to understand on the outside but inside she has a heart of gold.'

'Thank you for that, Bishop. Is there anything else I should know?'

'There is another sister . . . Sister Emma. She hasn't been with the order very long. She's still in her twenties, I believe. It's all in her file. She has a chequered history. Her mother, Vera, was a valued servant of God. She was a member of the same order, a very promising novice. The reports I've heard suggest her contemporaries believed she would become an example of how a life of poverty, chastity and obedience should be lived. However, one day, she was unexpectedly rushed to hospital, where it was discovered she was with child. She was soon delivered of a beautiful baby girl, Emma. The baby was adopted and Vera returned to the order; however, she never recovered her good health. She received special dispensation to leave the order, built up a relationship with her daughter and kept up her charitable life working in care homes and the like until she died in her late fifties. Emma was brought up in the Christian tradition, applied to be a sister in this order and here she is.'

Angel smiled. 'Anything else you should tell me, Bishop?'

'No . . . I think that's all, Inspector.'

Angel stood up. 'Thank you for that, Bishop.'

The other man took the hint and stood up.

They shook hands warmly. The Bishop clasped Angel's right hand and said, 'May God go with you.'

With a flourish of his cloak, the Bishop left.

As the door closed, Angel frowned and closed his eyes while he thought over all the Bishop had said. After a minute or two, he glanced at the computer screen, then his list of jobs. He picked up his mobile and rang DS Carter.

'Flora,' he said. 'We have not yet seen the woman who runs the bed and breakfast in Tunistone where Father Morgan was staying.'

'That's right — Mrs Jago,' Carter said.

'Will you phone her and see if she'll be in if we go up there to her now? It looks as if we may be able to save time, as our friends parked up at the front of the Feathers are seemingly not inclined to move.'

* * *

When Angel and Carter arrived at the bed and breakfast in Angel's BMW, Mrs Jago was at the door ready to meet them.

She was in a dress with a busy floral pattern. She was straight up and down, without an ounce of fat on her. Her hair was flat to her head and covered by a hairnet. She had a big mouth and big teeth. And, like her house, she was scrubbed spotlessly clean.

'You must be the police,' she said. 'Come on in, then. Wipe your feet. I hope you don't smoke. I don't allow smoking in the house.' She showed them into a small sitting room. 'Sit down wherever you like, except *that* chair,' she said, pointing to an easy chair in front of the fireplace. 'I always sit there.'

When they were seated, she said, 'Well, I must say, it's taken you long enough to come and see me, considering I was looking after the Reverend Morgan that fateful day. He only stayed one full night and, well, he died — God rest his soul — on the second. I don't know whether it would be reasonable to expect payment for that. I shall have to bill the Church something — there was a special price for clergy. Also, if a guest wished it, I prepared and served a hot evening meal at a mutually agreed time. On Saturday night the Reverend Morgan had — and I know he enjoyed it, because he said so — steak and kidney pie, carrots, stewed figs and custard, and coffee. I found him to be a most agreeable gentleman . . . very clean.'

'Thank you, Mrs Jago,' Angel said. 'I have a few questions I would like to ask you. Do you run this B & B on your own or does your husband help you?'

'Glory be, Inspector. I don't have a husband. Mr Jago left me over twenty years ago now. And I haven't heard from him since. I don't know what's happened to him. I expect he'll be dead by the way he was going on. No. I do everything myself and I rarely have vacancies. The Reverend Morgan was lucky. I had a cancellation from a young couple from Portsmouth that morning.'

Angel nodded. 'Did you know the Reverend Richard Morgan before he stayed with you on the twelfth of November?'

'No, not until he phoned a few days before and booked for Saturday and Sunday. I remember wondering if he was going to be the replacement priest that was going to perform services at the convent. If only he had been able to take over the running of the place, too — they need someone intelligent to step up there. You can see that. And they were very anxious to have a priest to take their confessions. And it turned out that I was absolutely correct.'

Angel frowned. 'Do you think the convent is not well run?'

'Of course it isn't,' Mrs Jago said. 'If it was, they wouldn't be so hard up. I gather that sometimes those women don't have enough food on the table. Well, I mean that Sister Julia was only a bit of a lass, wasn't she? Couldn't be more than forty or so . . . And what did she know about running a home and managing money? Nothing, I tell you. Her father is a lord and rolling in money. When Sister Precious was Reverend Mother they didn't have any problems at all. The convent ran like clockwork.'

'Do you know of anyone who didn't like the Reverend Mother?'

'Well, she never did me any favours . . . but we got on all right the very few times we spoke on the phone or met in church.'

'And how did Mr Morgan seem to be at breakfast on Sunday morning?'

'He was pleasant, charming . . . just as he'd been the night before.'

Angel was fast becoming aware that Mrs Jago had nothing else to add to their enquiries.

'Thank you, Mrs Jago,' he said. Then he turned to Carter. 'Right, let's go, Flora. Let's see if that car has moved.'

It was dark when they came out of Mrs Jago's. Angel looked at his watch. It was ten to five.

Carter had been keeping tabs on Brown's car via an app on her mobile; the screen showed a road map with a blue marker representing Brown's car. It was heading north-east out of Bromersley towards an area of mostly B roads through farmland, with the occasional hamlet here and there.

'They're on the move, sir,' she said.

Angel's pulse began to race. His mouth went dry. His eyes gleamed.

He smiled as he bounced into the car. 'Looks like we're working late tonight, Flora.'

'I don't mind. It'll be good to see Brown and Co. behind bars.'

Angel nodded in agreement as he let in the clutch and the car pulled away.

It was five o'clock when Angel and Carter arrived back at the police station.

Angel switched on his PC, and as the screen was coming up, he turned to Carter. 'Better grab Ted Scrivens before he leaves, Flora.'

She rushed out of the office.

Angel looked at the screen. The blue marker showed that Brown's car was still on the move along B roads in the middle of an area of farmland. Then the car passed the Ma Perkins Café and took a left turn.

Carter and Scrivens came into the office.

All three gathered round the computer screen.

Then suddenly Carter said, 'I think the car has stopped.'

Angel's face brightened. He peered at the screen. 'Yes. At a little place called Beden.'

Carter said, 'What do we do now, sir?'

'We wait.'

TEN

The following morning, Thursday, 24 November, before Angel got out of bed, he picked up his mobile from the bedside table, checked on the position of Brown's car and was pleased to find that it was still in Beden.

In his office two hours later, his PC showed him that the car had still not moved. So he pulled the pile of paperwork on his desk towards him and began looking through it.

He hadn't got far when DS Taylor came in, carrying a file. 'Have you a minute, sir? I've just got an email from the lab. Preliminary result from the forensics on the bedclothes and face of the Reverend Mother.'

Angel's eyebrows went up. 'Yes, Don. Come in. Sit down.'

Taylor opened the file. 'It's almost a copy of the results we had from the priest, Richard Morgan.'

'What? If I remember correctly, victim's own skin, resin, beeswax and charcoal.'

'Yes, sir . . . and two lengths of hair of South Asian origin.'

Angel looked ahead at nothing for a second then said, 'It adds strength to the contention that the same person murdered both victims. But I can't understand the presence of hair of South Asian origin. Nor the resin.'

Suddenly, Angel reached forward, picked up the phone, scrolled down the list of phone numbers and tapped on one.

The phone rang out.

A small voice answered. 'The Convent of the Reliquary of the Finger of Saint Ethel. Sister Precious speaking. How can I help you?'

'Inspector Angel here, Sister. Good morning. I'm looking among the nuns' files for one who might have South Asian heritage. I realise this is a slightly unusual question, but such things are not always obvious, especially when things like hair colour are hidden by religious vestments. Can you tell me if any of the present sisters have any South Asian heritage? The Indian subcontinent, I mean?'

'So far as I have observed, Inspector, our current members, such as they are, are all white. But you have their records. The answers you seek should be in them. Of course, this order has had nuns over the years from many different backgrounds.'

'I see. One more question, if I may . . . do you or any members of the community play a musical instrument?'

'I don't, and I am not aware that anyone here is musically gifted.'

'Thank you, Sister.'

'God bless you and keep you safe.'

* * *

It was ten o'clock that night.

Angel was driving, Carter was in the seat next to him navigating and Scrivens was in the back seat.

They came up to a mass of lights and a neon sign that read 'Ma Perkins'. It was a cosy transport café next to a small car park partly filled with commercial vehicles as well as private cars.

'Slow down, sir,' Carter said. 'There should be a left turning somewhere round here.'

They had travelled another five hundred yards or so when she said, 'There it is. The road sign says Beden's in one mile.'

Angel pulled to the side of the road and switched off the headlights. 'We'll stop here,' he said. 'We have to find our target without advertising our presence with headlights and engine noises. We'll go ahead on foot.'

'Right, sir,' she said.

He turned to Scrivens in the back. 'Look after the car, Ted. But don't nod off. I know its late. Be alert. I'll phone you soon.'

'Right, sir.'

Angel and Carter set off along the quiet, desolate road. The moon illuminated vast areas of cultivated land with very few hedges. There were no vehicles and no pedestrians, so they walked in the middle of the road.

As they walked, Angel said, 'We're approaching the village, Flora. We mustn't speak or make any noise.'

It was not long before they reached a small built-up area lit by sparse, dim streetlights. It had to be Beden. It was very quiet — the detectives could only hear the swirl of the wind and the occasional hoot of an owl. The village began with rows of small stone-built terraced houses on both sides of the road. They led to several larger houses that, judging from the size of their windows, had once been shops. There was a pub on the corner.

Miming directions to one another now and then, they went straight over the crossroads and past the village shop, which was next to a few more terraced houses. Then they came across a thick Leylandii hedge and wooden gates two metres high. Angel found a slight gap between the gates. He squinted through it and saw a brick-built detached house, lit dimly by an ornamental lantern, with an integral garage. It was more modern than the other houses they had seen in the village.

Angel grabbed Carter's sleeve, pointed to the gap in the gates and whispered, 'Take a look through there, Flora. If I could see the car in the garage, I would know if it was them.'

Carter peered through the gap in the doors and whispered, 'Yes. It's a possibility.'

Angel nodded eagerly. 'I'm going up, Flora. You stay here.'

Carter said, 'OK,' and she gave him her torch.

Angel carefully opened one of the tall drive gates and walked noiselessly up the drive to the house, which was as silent as death. He looked up at the windows. In the limited light they were all dark grey. He couldn't detect whether they were curtained or not.

He went straight to the garage door to see if there was a handle. It didn't need one: it was operated by a remote and it was locked. Then he went round the side of the house, where he was glad to find a window. He flashed the torch briefly through the window into the garage. He saw the bonnet of the big car, and if he went to one side, he could just see the number plate. AHE 156. *That* was the one.

He grinned from ear to ear. His eyes sparkled. He glanced upwards and mouthed, 'Thank you.' Then he rushed back down the drive to tell Carter.

Angel was unaware that from a window above the garage, a pair of eyes had been watching him.

'That's the car all right,' Angel whispered. 'Let's get away from here. We've taken enough risks.'

Carter agreed. They quickly walked back about a hundred metres to the crossroads, then Angel opened his mobile, scrolled down to a number and clicked on it.

'Ted,' he whispered. 'We've found the target. Come down the road *quietly* as you can . . . don't use your lights unless you have to . . . you'll see some crossroads . . . go across them . . . you'll see us on the corner on your left. Be as quiet as you can. All right?'

Angel pocketed his mobile and rubbed his hands to keep them warm. All was silent except for the hoot of an owl.

'I hate waiting,' Angel whispered.

Carter nodded.

Then they heard the noise of a car engine. It was getting louder . . . and it wasn't coming from the direction they were expecting. It was coming from behind them . . . from the direction of Brown's house.

With open mouths, they turned then glanced at each other.

There was a loud bang, and Brown's car crashed through the gate, throwing bits of wood and splinters in the air.

Angel said, 'Take cover!'

Angel and Carter dropped down on to the pavement.

Powerful spotlights shone through the open car windows and a shower of gunshots rapidly fired in every direction. Pieces of the gate slid off the car's bonnet.

The car careered out into the road, rocked uncertainly on two wheels before it righted itself, shed more pieces of the wooden gate onto the road and raced away. In seconds the car was out of sight and earshot.

Angel said, 'Are you all right?'

'Yes,' Carter said.

Angel didn't like to see Brown and company getting away. He looked anxiously ahead. 'Where's Scrivens? Where's my car?'

Angel's BMW glided slowly across the crossroads.

Around the hamlet, five or six bedroom windows were now illuminated. He could hear voices. More windows were being lit up by the second. He wasn't surprised. The racket Brown made would have awakened the dead.

He ran to the car. 'I'll drive, Ted. Quick, get in the back. Jump in, Flora.'

Angel had to travel over big chunks of the wrecked gate before the road ahead was clear. When he reached a speed much more than the law allowed, he said, 'Flora, where is Brown's car now?'

Carter already had the map with the blue marker on screen.

'I've got it,' she said, then blinked at what she found.

'Tell me which way to turn, Flora.'

'They seem to have travelled a good distance in a very short space of time.'

Angel sighed noisily. 'Are we on the way to catch them, Flora . . . or are we not?'

'They're on the M1, sir.'

Angel's jaw dropped. 'Are they really? Are you following the blue flashing marker?'

'Yes, of course. We're travelling in the right direction, but not the route they must have taken. Carry on along this road and we'll soon be on the M1.'

Angel nodded and hoped that Carter knew what she was doing.

Soon afterwards the sign to the M1 came up and Angel turned left up the slip road. The M1 was certainly fast-moving. They passed a sign that confirmed they were travelling north towards Carlisle.

Then Carter said, 'We're less than five miles behind Brown's car.'

Angel's careful but forceful driving soon caught them up — with a fish delivery truck. It was the vehicle that seemed to be emitting the signal that Carter was reading and Angel was following.

With the aid of a flashing light placed temporarily on the roof of the BMW and an ear-splitting siren, Angel stopped the driver on the hard shoulder. Angel soon found the tracker fastened with brown tape to the underside of a mud guard on the wheel of the smelly fish truck.

They had been tricked.

The driver seemed innocent enough, and when he told Angel that his last stop had been for a meal at Ma Perkins, Angel knew what had happened.

The tracker had been found on Brown's car, taken off and stuck on to the vilest vehicle they could find, just to show off and waste police time.

Angel grudgingly took the tracker, waved the driver of the fish truck off and got back into the BMW.

He was very quiet during the drive back.

* * *

It was 3.30 a.m. when he put his key into the back door of his bungalow.

He was tired but he was also hungry. And thirsty. He licked his lips. He could drink a gallon of tea. But everywhere would be closed. Even the chip shop.

And Mary was still in Edinburgh. The house was lonely, quiet and cold. There was no one to hug, kiss and talk to.

He needed something hot and tasty on a plate. He wanted something that needed minimum effort and time to produce. It had to be good old beans on toast and a mug of tea.

He was soon at the worktop in the kitchen in dressing gown and slippers.

Five minutes later he mashed the tea, dished up the toast and the beans, sat down at the table and attacked his meal with a knife and fork. After a while he reached out for the tea. He took a sip, said, 'Ah,' approvingly and took several more.

When he had cleared the toast, beans and tea, he went to bed and fell asleep almost immediately. It was the sleep of the innocent.

At about 4.30 a.m., there was the sound of a loud crash and the clatter of broken glass.

He immediately sat up in bed, awake and alert. He listened in the dark. He found himself breathing hard and fast.

The noise seemed to have come from the spare bedroom.

Then he heard a car door slam shut, an engine rev up and a squeal of tyres as the vehicle was quickly driven away.

He jumped out of bed, went into the hall and along to the spare bedroom. He opened the door and switched on the light. On the carpet between the wardrobe and the bed, right in front of him, was a red house brick with an envelope stuck to it with sticky tape. The window was smashed to pieces, and shards of glass were scattered around the window ledge and carpet.

He was glad Mary hadn't been here to see this. It would have unnerved her. She would have had a fit. It would have started her on the argument about the unacceptable dangers of being a policeman, and that he should get a job as a teacher or a bank clerk or a dustbin man. Although he missed her, he was pleased that she was in Edinburgh, where she would be safe from Brown and Smith. There was the added advantage that he didn't have to be in the company of Miriam, which would have upset and annoyed him no end.

He reached down to the brick and pulled off the envelope. Inside was a single sheet of paper.

It read:

Angel.

We have told you before to stop following us. If you don't, and something serious happuns to you, it won't be our fault.

You have been warned.

Best Insurance Company.

It was a threat. *What did you expect?* Angel thought. He was tiring of chasing Brown and Smith and Moss up and down. It really was time he had the three of them in prison.

Later that morning, he would get the window fixed and get it all cleaned up before Mary returned. She needn't know anything about it.

* * *

That Friday morning, after Lauds, Sister Precious and Sister Emma went out of the back gate of the convent, crossed the road and walked a little way to visit their tenant, Mr Max Diamond, who had a vehicle repair business on the ground floor of the huge stone building known as Duxbury Mill.

Sister Precious led the way to the office — she had been many times before — and knocked on the door.

'Come in,' he called.

Diamond was sitting at his desk. He stood up and smiled at the older nun as they entered. 'How nice to see you, Sister Precious. Please sit down. What can I do for you? I'm so sorry to hear that the Reverend Mother has been, erm, taken from you. You must tell me the day of the funeral.'

Then his eyes lit upon Emma. He gazed at her and smiled even more widely.

Sister Precious said, 'Thank you, Mr Diamond. I'm afraid that we are still waiting for the police to release her body, so for now that decision is out of our hands. I am here today to ask you for more practical assistance. I know the rent is payable monthly and not yet due, but we are out of funds and I am here to ask you if you would be kind enough to pay us the proportion of this month that you have occupied the premises . . . if you understand me?'

'I do understand you, Sister Precious, and I can certainly do that. In the meantime, please tell me: what is the name of this beautiful young lady?'

Emma blushed and looked downward.

There was a pause.

Precious looked down her nose at the man with the expression of someone hovering over a cesspit. 'She is not a lady, Mr Diamond. She is a nun. Her name is Sister Emma. She is the youngest and one of the most devoted in our ever-depleting numbers.'

'Delightful,' he said, still looking and smiling at Emma.

Precious quickly produced a small piece of paper. 'I have worked out the proportion to date . . . you can see what it amounts to.' She handed him the paper.

He reluctantly took it and was obliged to stop gazing at Emma and look down. When the financial business was over, the two nuns thanked Diamond and quickly went out of his office.

Precious felt very much happier with a bundle of ten-pound notes in the capacious pocket of her habit.

They made for the back door of the convent, where there was a small laundry — the washing and pressing machines had been installed long ago, when the number of members of the order was very much higher.

Sister Clare and Sister Teresa were busy among the steam and the rattling of the old machines, using wooden tongs to transfer hot, wet linen sheets from a large soaking tub used for lightly bleaching to a washing machine. It required patience and some strength to unravel and lift the wet, heavy blankets.

The door was open. Precious went into the steam and pother, and Emma followed.

Precious caught Clare's attention, and above the noise and commotion she called, 'I collected some rent money from Mr Diamond.'

Clare looked at Emma, who nodded. Clare pointed to the machine then put a hand to her ear. Emma understood and shut off the machines.

Teresa looked across in surprise.

The silence was a welcome relief to everybody.

Clare dropped the tongs in the water. 'I couldn't hear you.'

'I collected some rent money from Mr Diamond. Emma and I will go to the supermarket and get some groceries. Today, we can have a proper supper. I thought you would be pleased.'

'I am pleased,' Clare replied, 'but who gave you the right, the authority, to speak to Mr Diamond? We didn't discuss this. You're not Reverend Mother. What makes you think you're in charge?'

Teresa added, 'I know you're the eldest, Precious, but it doesn't give you any authority over us.'

Precious breathed in and out heavily and stood her full height. 'I don't *think* I'm in charge. I just happen to be the one who *knows* what to do, and furthermore I am doing it. I have done it for thirty years. It has become second nature. If you want to do it, please do it. I don't seek this responsibility.'

Clare said, 'The appointment should be made by the Bishop.'

'I agree,' Teresa said.

'What about a ballot?' Emma suggested. 'Just until the Bishop makes up his mind, we do need somebody to keep things ticking over. We could do that here and now. Stop all this bickering and time-wasting. There's only the four of us.'

'I am not bickering,' Precious said. 'May the good Lord forgive me if I am. I am just stating the situation and the facts as they are.'

Clare said, 'Never mind all that, Sister Precious, are you agreeable to a ballot or not?'

'Provided that it is understood that we are we doing this as an emergency temporary measure until we can prevail upon Bishop Letterman.'

Clare said, 'Yes, which might take some time.'

'Whatever do you mean?'

'Whenever I phone him lately, he's away at concerts.'

'He works *very* hard.' Precious sounded as if she was close to losing her patience. 'Every one of God's servants is allowed interests and hobbies. Is your answer yes or no?'

'All right,' Clare said. 'I agree. Yes.'

Then Precious saw Emma was looking thoughtful.

'Is this ballot all right with you, Emma?'

Emma was looking ahead at nothing. Her mind had reverted to Mr Diamond, his tanned face and arms, his kindness, his charm, his constant gaze upon her and his words . . . 'What is the name of this *beautiful young lady*?' Diamond was the third man who had told her that she was *beautiful*. She liked it. It was terrific . . . fabulous . . . and prideful. She had feelings for him she shouldn't have as a nun. The guilt made her feel uncomfortable.

On hearing Clare saying her name, Emma came straight back to the convent and the laundry.

'Sorry, I was, er . . . thinking.'

'I said, is a ballot all right with you?' Precious repeated.

'Oh? Well, it was my idea, so if that is the view of everybody, yes, of course.'

Clare said, 'What shall we do? Names in a hat?'

'Yes, and let us all ask for the guidance of the Holy Spirit in making this decision,' Precious rejoined quickly.

'We want four pieces of paper and four pencils,' Teresa said.

Emma was back to the here and now. 'I'll get them from the office.'

ELEVEN

It was Saturday, 26 November.

The incessant ringing of the phone at the side of Angel's bed roused him from a very deep, dreamless sleep.

He reached out for the handset and noticed that he was wearing a shirt and trousers covered by a dressing gown, and that he was on top of the duvet, also that the bedside light was on.

He glanced at the clock. It was 9.30 a.m. He blinked.

He must have fallen asleep.

Then it all came back to him. He had been up half the night investigating another horrible murder at the convent. He had slipped home for a shower and a shave and something quick and easy to eat. He must have rested on the bed for a moment and simply dropped off. That would have been five hours ago.

He put the phone to his cheek.

'Yeah? Who is it?'

'It's me,' the woman said. 'Darling, have I woken you up?'

It was Mary.

'Oh, sweetheart . . . No, of course not. I was just clearing the breakfast pots in the kitchen. How are you? Is everything all right?'

'I was worried about you. I haven't heard from you since Wednesday.'

'Well, I've been very busy with work, you know.'

'Are you looking after yourself, regular meals, in bed by ten and all that?'

'Oh yes, yes, yes. It's a piece of cake. Is Miriam all right?'

'Sends her love. She says that she's disappointed you didn't come with me.'

Angel shook his head and grinned. 'I *bet* she is.'

'And she wants to know if you can manage without me for another four days?'

Angel thought that would fit in very nicely. He wanted to have Brown and his gang behind bars and the case neatly wrapped up before Mary returned and provided Brown with an easy target for him and his evil little gang.

Angel had to think quickly. 'Oh, I dunno,' he said slowly.

'It's doing Miriam an awful lot of good . . . and I am feeling the wonderful benefits of the fresh air and walks by the sea in Leith. Of course, darling, if you can't manage, I—'

'No, love. You stay where you are,' he said quickly. 'I miss you terribly, but if you and Miriam are feeling the benefit . . .'

'Oh thank you, darling. I'll go and tell her. She'll be as over the moon as I am. I'll ring you again soon. Lots of love. Bye.'

He smiled as he returned the phone to its holster.

Then he raced round, shaved, had a good wash, changed his shirt, made some toast and a big mug of tea, gobbled it down and raced out to the car.

* * *

It was eleven o'clock that Saturday morning when a weary Angel and a slightly less weary Carter stood in front of the three surviving members of the convent in the sitting room.

Sister Teresa had been murdered in the night, discovered by Sister Precious early the next morning, and Angel had been duly notified. The *modus operandi* was the same as with the Reverend Mother.

'Sisters,' Angel began, 'Detective Sergeant Carter and I have examined the evidence, read and re-read your statements and reached an unavoidable conclusion. You all three say that the convent doors and windows were all closed, locked and checked last night at around seven o'clock. We have examined them most closely, and there are no signs that they have been broken or forced open. The pathologist estimates the time of death of Sister Teresa at around midnight. Therefore, access to the victim could only be achieved by one or more of you three, so very regretfully I have to say that one of you must be the murderer.'

The three women looked at each other in surprise.

Sister Precious said, 'Inspector Angel, I do not take exception to you accusing me of such an act. Perhaps you think I'm capable of such evil. But I do take exception to you accusing my dear sisters of such wickedness. As temporary Reverend Mother in this house, I really must defend my two dear sisters, who have surrendered many material pleasures for spiritual and holy disciplines. It is inconceivable that either of them could even *think* of murdering another person.'

'With respect, Sister Precious, forensic evidence indicates that the same sister also murdered the priest, Richard Morgan, and your own Reverend Mother by inflicting a similar wound directly into the heart, using the same or an identical weapon.

'I have a warrant to search these premises and your good selves. The upstairs rooms are currently being searched by SOC officers. You will be personally searched by women officers who are on their way from the station. I would ask you to remain in this room here under the care of DS Carter until the officers arrive.'

The room door opened.

Angel turned, eyebrows raised.

It was DS Taylor. His eyes gleamed. 'Can I have a quiet word?' he said softly.

Angel nodded.

Taylor came up close and quietly said, 'We've found a stiletto in a holster at the back of a picture hanging from the wall in the room known as Saint Peter's. It still has dried blood on it.'

Angel stomach bounced. 'Any prints?'

'Several on the picture. Haven't dusted the holster and stiletto. Sooner do that at the station.'

Carter came across to Angel. 'Found something?'

Angel whispered the news.

'Saint Peter's is Sister Precious's room,' she said.

Angel frowned at the information.

'I'll come straightaway, Don.' To Carter, he said, 'Will you stay with these three sisters, Flora?' Then he added more quietly, 'Watch them very carefully. One of them has already murdered three times.'

The muscles in Carter's body tightened. She delicately licked her lips.

* * *

Angel followed Don Taylor into Sister Precious's room. It was very small, with an old, black iron bed with large, ugly castors on a polished wooden floor, a simple bedside table, a cupboard, a wardrobe and plain white walls with three different black-and-white prints of Saint Peter on separate walls. Above the bedhead was a plain wooden cross.

Taylor pulled on his rubber gloves and made for the wall directly opposite the cross, then reached up to unhook the picture from a nail. A ridge behind the picture was sufficient to hold the stiletto and holster safely in position and out of sight when the picture was hanging against the wall. Taylor had to hold the picture face down and level so as not to allow the stiletto and holster to slide and drop onto the floor. He lowered it to show Angel what they had found.

Angel rubbed his chin. 'That certainly looks like the weapon. It's possible that there are prints in the smears of dried blood. Mmm. Will you put it back as you found it for the time being?'

'Right, sir.'

'How tall are you, Don?'

Taylor screwed up his face. 'Six foot three. Why?'

With a wrinkled brow Angel shook his head. 'Just wondered.'

Taylor's eyes narrowed. He was thinking. Angel never did or said anything without a reason.

'Have you finished in here?' Angel said.

'Yes, sir.'

Angel went back downstairs to the sitting room.

The three sisters and DS Carter were seated in the easy chairs.

'Carter, I want to borrow Sister Precious, if you don't mind.'

Sister Precious, on hearing her name, looked across at him.

Angel put out a hand indicating that he wanted her to come with him.

'Thank you,' he said.

They went upstairs.

When they reached Precious's room, he stood back by the door, put on a pair of rubber gloves and said, 'Do you like being in this particular room?'

'It is a great honour to be in a room dedicated to Saint Peter,' she said. 'He is the one disciple that Christ directed to build his Church. In a very small way, that's what I have endeavoured to do.'

He went across to the picture concealing the weapon, reached up and carefully unhooked it, tilted it forward so that the weapon didn't slide on to the floor, lowered it and showed it to Precious.

'Look what we've found.'

As soon as she recognised what she was seeing, she took a sharp intake of breath. 'The stiletto!' she said.

Then she turned away from it, closed her eyes and kneeled down in a prayerful position.

Angel put the picture bearing the holster and stiletto down on the bed.

Then he turned back to her. Soon she stood up.

'We believe it was the one used to murder Father Morgan, the Reverend Mother and Sister Teresa, yes,' he said. 'The strange question I have to ask is how do you account for it being concealed behind this picture here in *your* room?'

There was no reply for a few seconds. Then she said, 'I would ask you to notify Bishop Letterman of this turn of events.'

'He can be . . . after this interview, Sister. But how did this stiletto find its way here?'

'No comment,' Sister Precious said in a very small voice.

Angel put a hand up to his forehead and wiped it slowly down his face to his chin. 'Does that mean you *don't* know or that you *do* know but are unwilling to say?'

'No comment.'

Angel wrinkled his nose. He hadn't expected Sister Precious to be so unhelpful. He didn't think she was a murderer. Yet sometimes she behaved as if she was.

'Are you going to say "no comment" to anything I say to you from now on?'

She thought for a moment. 'Probably.'

Angel sniffed. At least that last answer broke the monotony.

Still wearing the rubber gloves, he took a pencil out of his top pocket and a polythene bag out of his inside pocket. He opened the bag and held it open. Then he pushed the pencil into a loop at the top of the holster and lifted it off the back of the picture.

At that point he said, 'Would you put that picture back up for me, Sister?'

She nodded.

Out of his eye corner he watched her. At the same time, he gently manoeuvred the holster and stiletto into the bag.

She picked up the picture and held it up to the wall as high as she could and looked upward. She was about a foot too short. She looked round her room. So did he. There was nothing to stand on.

Angel took out his pen, wrote on a label on the polythene bag and put it in his pocket.

Precious went out on to the landing, muttering away. Angel followed her into the room next door, Saint Paul's.

'Where are you going, Sister?'

'Oh. Looking for something to, er . . . stand on,' she said, 'a chair.'

'I'll do it. I can reach. Come back in here.'

Angel stretched up, returned the picture of Saint Peter and checked that it was level.

His mobile rang. He opened it up. It was DC Scrivens. Angel said, 'Yes, Ted?'

'Have you heard what's happened at Levi's antiques shop, sir?'

Angel sighed. He knew it would be trouble.

'No, what?'

'Seems a fire started in the shop, during the night. I thought you'd want to know.'

Angel gasped. His skin tingled.

'Right. Anybody hurt?'

'Don't know, sir.'

'What caused it?'

'Don't know. Only just heard the fire service was turned out.'

'Thanks, Ted.'

He put away his mobile. He had a heavy feeling in his stomach.

He quickly took Sister Precious down to the sitting room, where the other two sisters and DS Carter were welcoming the three women police officers who had just arrived.

He caught Carter's eye. 'Carry on here, Flora. Got to go.' Then in a whisper he added, 'Watch those three nuns. Be careful.'

Before she could say anything he was outside the front door of the convent.

Levi's Antiques was at the other side of the town, on the corner of Market Street and Scargill Street. He drove straight down the main road into the town centre and then along King Street.

There was already the smell of smoke.

Angel had a sour taste in his mouth.

He closed the car window.

As he turned into Market Street he saw that the road ahead was blocked by 'No Entry' signs; the air was a foggy blue. He parked the car where it was and put a 'Police on Duty' card in the window.

He wondered about the Levis and their children, and his heart felt heavy.

As he turned the corner he saw the burnt-out shop and house. Every part of the building that was combustible — furniture, window frames, doors, floorboards — had been consumed by the fire, whereas the bricks and mortar, tiles and stone were relatively intact. There were thick black smoke marks on the bricks round some of the windows, and there was the sound of water trickling out of the building across the pavement, along the gutters to the drains. There was no sign of any flames but there were frequent thin lines of white smoke rising.

Eight firefighters were standing in front of a fire engine looking towards the burnt-out building, talking among themselves and drinking tea.

Angel approached them producing his warrant card and holding it up to those who were interested. 'Excuse me. Is there any news about the family who lived here?'

One of them said, 'The whole family were taken off to hospital with smoke inhalation. The woman was in a bad way.'

Angel nodded. 'What started the fire?'

'Molotov cocktail — it came through the shop window.'

'What time was this?'

'We was turned out at midnight. We was the first to arrive and the last to leave . . . and we haven't gone yet.' The firefighter looked at his watch. 'And it's one o'clock! My dinner time.'

Angel gave a gentle wave. 'I won't delay you, then. Thank you.'

He went straight to Bromersley General Hospital. The lady on the Enquiries Desk told him that Ruth Levi had been admitted in the night and that she was on ward fourteen, third floor.

He quickly made his way up there.

When the lift doors opened he saw Mr Levi, still in pyjamas and overcoat, sitting on his own in a waiting area of about twelve seats outside the ward. Levi seemed to have shrunk since Angel had last seen him — his head was bowed, and he was looking towards the floor. His shoulders drooped and he was clutching his stomach. As Angel walked in, Levi slowly turned towards the open lift doors. Their eyes met. He sighed, as if relieved to see a friendly face, and stood up unsteadily as Angel approached him. His face was pale and his eyes were bloodshot.

'Oh . . . Inspector,' Levi said.

'Sit down. Sit down.'

They shook hands heartily. Levi was reluctant to release his hand.

'I was sorry to hear about the fire. How's your wife?'

Levi shook his head and swallowed. His jaw trembled. 'Burns . . . all over her body. Waiting to hear.'

Angel gave an understanding nod. He was again thankful that Mary was still in Edinburgh.

'So she's going to be all right?' Angel said brightly.

Levi's jaw trembled. 'D-d-don't know.'

'And your children, are they all right?'

'Yes,' he said. 'They're at their grandmother's.'

'That's *great*,' Angel said with a forced smile. 'And what about you?'

Levi took in a big breath. 'I'm all right. I'm learning.'

Angel screwed up his face. 'What do you mean?'

'Every day I'm learning.'

'I suppose we're all learning . . .'

'I'm learning how to live, Inspector. My eyes have been opened. I've learned not to trust a word that Brown says. He promised me that, provided I paid him . . . But you know all that, Inspector.'

'Did you pay him after our visit to your shop?'

'I was scared, Inspector. I paid him more. A lot more. He was coming every day. I began to realise that what you said was right. But it was too late. I actually ran out of cash. It wasn't that I wouldn't pay him, I simply *couldn't* pay him. He thought I was holding back. He was furious, he threatened to set fire to my shop. This was his revenge.'

Angel nodded. 'Did he actually *say* he would set fire to the shop?'

'Oh, yes. He had said it more than once. Why is he so difficult to catch, Inspector?'

Angel pursed his lips. 'He moves fast, he doesn't take risks and he's been lucky.'

The lift doors suddenly opened, and they looked in their direction.

A stooping lady in her late fifties hobbled out of the lift on to the landing.

'It's Ruth's mother,' Levi said.

She came straight up to him, ignoring the detective. 'How is Ruth?'

'Excuse me,' Angel said. 'I'll leave you in the very capable hands of your mother-in-law, Mr Levi. I have a lot I must do.'

'Yes, of course. Thank you, Inspector.'

'Goodbye.' Angel pressed the button to call the lift.

* * *

That afternoon, Angel emailed all the men and women in the force in plain clothes and all uniformed officers on the afternoon shift that were not on essential duties to assemble in the order room at sixteen hundred hours.

He was there to greet them. He told them that it was an informal meeting and to take a chair from the neat stack at the back and sit down anywhere. He counted them. There were eighteen, twelve men and six women. He had hoped for around twenty-four.

The clock chimed four, so he began.

'I've gathered you here today urgently to report the latest outrage of the conman Ezra Brown, and his associates Reg Smith and the man we know only as "Moss".

'Not long ago they threatened a shopkeeper that they would burn down his business if he didn't pay. He couldn't pay. At about midnight last night, the building where his family was sleeping was burned down. The mother is in hospital in a critical condition.

'Brown and his sidekicks are an evil nuisance to this town and its time they were locked up. We've dallied about with these characters too long.

'So this evening I want you to visit every pub, restaurant, hotel and bar and tell staff to promptly call the police if they see any of those three characters.

'Now, DS Carter is allocating areas for each of you, please see her. And DC Scrivens is distributing leaflets giving revised descriptions of the wanted men. Take as many as you need.

'Thank you. That is all.'

TWELVE

It was Sunday, 27 November. Angel woke up and looked at the clock. It said ten to nine. After a moment or two, he pushed down the duvet, sat up, swivelled round, put his feet on the floor and pulled on his slippers. He yawned, then stretched his arms.

He wondered what Mary was doing. Probably walking on a beach somewhere with Miriam's dog. He smiled. Wrapped up wearing a snood that enhanced her pretty face, made her look like some multi-million-dollar film star trying to hide from the media and her adoring public.

After a few moments, he sniffed, dragged on his dressing gown and shuffled into the kitchen.

He made some toast and tea, and switched on the television for company. It was now just after nine o'clock so the news was on. It seemed to be all about the pros and cons of Brexit, and the prime minister's visit to Scotland. It was followed by the local news, which lead with an item about the three murders at the convent in Bromersley. There were pictures of the outside of the convent, filmed from the open front gate, then an old still photograph of the altar and the casket containing Saint Ethel's finger. That was followed by a report on the fire at the antiques shop in Market Street. That showed film of the fire and an ambulance with a stretcher case — it would be Mrs Levi — being carried and delivered safely to the vehicle and whisked away.

Angel shook his head. The circles he was compelled to move in were becoming more dangerous.

He demolished the last piece of toast, drained the last drop of tea in the pot then dashed outside. He looked around. Absolute silence. Nobody in sight. With a trowel from the tool shed, he recovered the green plastic bag from beneath the sunflowers. He went into the shed, unwrapped the Beretta, left the bag and trowel on the bench and returned to the kitchen.

He was determined to go into the station and see if there were any developments in either case.

He quickly washed, shaved and dressed, carefully transferring the Beretta from his dressing gown pocket to his jacket pocket.

He reversed the BMW out of the garage and drove out of the estate. There was little or no traffic about, being Sunday. He passed a white laundry van standing in a lay-by at the side of the road.

It was a short stretch to the ring road, from which it would take him only three or four minutes to reach the police station. However, as he reached the turning, a sign across it read 'Road Closed', so he had to take Dandelion Lane, which led through Bromersley Woods. There was no access to the ring road here, and he would have to travel through the town centre to reach the station. It would put one or two minutes on the trip. If it had been a weekday, it would have taken longer.

As he pulled the steering wheel to the left, in his mirror he could see a white van coming up fast behind him. He read the writing above the van's cab. It was in reverse but he worked out that it said 'Sheffield Sanitary Laundry'. Then he felt a slight bump and heard a scraping noise at the back of the car. The van had hit him.

'The fool!' Angel said angrily. He'd have to stop to see what damage had been done.

He looked in the mirror again and tried to see the driver.

He pressed his left indicator and slowed down.

The van began to overtake him. The driver seemed to have no intention of slowing down. Angel quickly responded by pressing down his right foot.

The BMW surged forward, leaving the white van to drop back and behind him.

Angel again looked into the mirror. The driver was a man and he was wearing sunglasses. There was no sign of the sun.

They were on a long straight road through the centre of the woods. By now, both vehicles were travelling at sixty or seventy miles an hour.

Angel spotted a gathering of three sheep chomping on a patch of something green and interesting on the verge ahead. The sheep spilled out dangerously on to the road, moving quickly around to the best spot to access their find.

Angel had to slow down.

The van pulled around him and drew level. The driver had removed his sunglasses and was holding a gun in his left hand.

Angel gasped.

It was Reg Smith.

Angel put his foot down on the accelerator to get out of his sights.

Smith fired two shots at Angel. He missed his target but one of the shots shattered the BMW's windscreen.

Angel punched the fragmented glass pieces out. The cold wind raced in.

He missed the sheep.

The BMW surged forward before Smith had the chance to take another shot.

The van pulled behind Angel just as a car came along the road towards them, as if to remind Smith that this was not a one-way road.

Angel took the Beretta out of his jacket pocket and put it on the seat at his side. He only wanted to defend himself.

He knew that if he killed anybody, even to protect himself or someone else, there would be the most unholy inquiry as to how he had come into the possession of a gun — the police are only allowed guns under very special conditions and only with permission from their superiors. He had asked for that permission and had been unequivocally denied.

The van quickly attempted to draw level with Angel again.

Angel allowed him to come so far, then he picked up his gun, and looking in his off-side mirror, he put his hand out of the window and fired rapidly down and back at the van's wheels. It took Angel four shots to hit the van's nearside front tyre.

The van immediately slowed, jerked to its left, went across the pavement, over the verge and hobbled down through some bushes into the woods.

There was a mighty crash.

Angel stopped the BMW and rushed back to the place where the van had left the road. He went down into the bushes and there it was. The van had been stopped in its tracks by a small cluster of mature silver birch.

The driver's door was swinging open. With the gun in his hand, he looked inside. There was no sign of Smith.

Angel assumed that the man was all right and somewhere in the woods, hiding or making for home.

Angel came quickly away. Disappointed, he sighed heavily and ran his hand through his hair. He made a quick look round just to check again if Smith was visible, then returned to his car.

He drove into the police vehicle pound at the back of the station, covered the big hole in the windscreen with a piece of canvas, then made his way through the rear door to the charge room. DS Clifton was on duty.

'Good morning, Bernie,' Angel said. 'Who's the duty transport engineer? I've got a shattered windscreen.'

'On a Sunday? Nobody, sir. Back tomorrow at eight o'clock. Did a pebble fly up?'

'Something like that,' Angel said. 'Give me the keys to the station car.'

Clifton turned to a keyboard behind him and passed the keys across the long counter. He produced a book, wrote something in it, turned it round and gave Angel the pen. Angel signed his name and returned the pen.

'Thank you, Bernie. Anything happening?'

'Pretty quiet for a change. We've had a couple of domestics. Both on Canal Street. A drunk causing a disturbance in the White Horse. And a delivery van taken without permission.'

'Oh yes? Are there any roadworks on our patch?'

'The bottom of Wakefield Road. There's always roadworks down there. We haven't been notified of any other.'

'What about Dandelion Lane, near where I live?'

'No. There's no pipes down there to dig up, is there?'

Angel shrugged. 'What about the stolen delivery van?'

'Yes. A driver for the Sheffield Sanitary Laundry brought the van home. He said it was taken while he was in the shower last night.'

Angel pursed his lips. 'Oh, really?'

* * *

On Monday morning, Angel was in his office re-reading the statements of the three remaining nuns at the convent when his mobile phone rang.

'This is police patrol car driver Donohue 297. Is that DI Angel?'

'Yes. Go ahead, Sean.'

'Are you still interested in that big old car, licence plate number Alpha Hotel Echo 156, sir?'

Angel stood up. 'Indeed I am, Sean,' he said quickly. 'Why?'

'I was surveying King Street looking for a particular stolen car when I saw this car, and its number rang a bell. So I looked in the records and there it was. It's parked in front of Helliwell's fish and chip shop.'

Angel felt like he had a fox and a dozen hens in his stomach.

'That's great, Sean. I know where you mean,' Angel said. 'Is there anyone in or around it?'

'No, sir.'

'Is it possible for you to surreptitiously let down one of their tyres . . . and make it seem like a puncture?'

'I'll try, sir,' Donohue said.

'The owner is dangerous, Sean. He and his accomplices are wanted for several offences and are known to be armed, so move away from the area ASAP. Don't take any risks.'

Angel closed the phone, ran to his car and drove like a fury to Bromersley town centre. His chest felt light and his mouth was dry.

King Street was busy with traffic and shoppers. He had to drive very slowly because he was behind a stream of vehicles. He soon saw Brown's car outside the chippie, next door to the old theatre. It had a puncture in its front nearside tyre. No sign of Brown or his accomplices.

Angel smiled. 'Good old Sean,' he muttered to himself.

He had to find a parking spot for his own car. He turned left alongside the old theatre. It was a quiet side street primarily used as a car park. Angel found a space halfway down and was much relieved. He turned off the engine and looked for some handcuffs under the dashboard. He found two pairs and took them both. He ambled back up the side street and wondered if he had time to phone for backup. Then he peered round the corner of the old theatre and saw Moss. He was standing at the front of the big car, looking at the flat tyre.

Angel breathed more deeply. His eyes glowed with inner light. He was standing only ten metres away.

Moss was now at the back of the car. He had the boot open and his head was in it, presumably looking for the tools to change the wheel.

Angel dashed out between shoppers to reach a position behind the man.

He pulled out the Beretta, stuck it in Moss's back, and said, 'This is DI Angel.'

Moss froze and stood erect. 'What do you want?'

'Put your hands behind your back.'

Moss hesitated then passed back both hands while clenching his jaw and grinding his teeth.

'I don't know what this is about,' he said. 'I'm only out here to do some shopping. I'm not doing anybody any harm. Just a few groceries.'

Angel pulled a pair of handcuffs out of his pocket and snapped a cuff over one of Moss's wrists. Angel then began to switch hands to more easily snap the cuffs around Moss's other wrist.

Moss suddenly pulled both his wrists away, whipped round and made a grab for the gun.

Angel held on to the Beretta and banged his free fist hard into Moss's temple. Moss blinked but still held a firm grip on the gun.

Angel repeated the blow but even harder.

Moss winced and released the hold he had on the gun.

Angel then managed to jab Moss's stomach with the barrel and said, 'Turn round. Put your hands behind your back. And don't try anything like that again.'

A few seconds later the other cuff was duly snapped around Moss's other wrist.

Angel closed the car boot, pocketed the Beretta and patted Moss down. He found a gun in his jacket pocket, a Smith & Wesson. He looked at the magazine. It was fully loaded. He checked the safety catch then put the gun in his pocket.

'Do you always go shopping carrying a gun?' Angel asked.

Then he marched Moss across the front of the theatre and round the corner to the parked cars. The side road was quiet. No pedestrians. He led him down to his BMW and left him standing facing the theatre wall while he ferreted about in his car boot. He came out with a length of rope ten or fifteen metres long. He threaded the rope around the handcuffs and made a secure knot.

'What you doing?' Moss said.

Angel opened the rear nearside door. 'Get in the car.'

'I can't sit comfortably with these cuffs.'

Angel was bitterly amused by the remark. 'Well, do the best you can.'

Then he threaded the rope through the hand grip above the door and pulled the rope through to the end.

'That's too tight!' Moss winced.

Angel pulled it another centimetre and Moss yelled an expletive.

Angel tied the rope off, and Moss sat on the front edge of the seat in an upright position. Every time he struggled, the rope tightened and the more uncomfortable he became.

Without cutting the rope, Angel carried the excess to the floor of the car and tied his ankles together.

Then he pulled a yellow duster out of a pocket in the door and put it across Moss's mouth and tied it tight behind his head.

Then he locked the car and made his way along the path at the side of the theatre back towards Brown's car. At the corner he stopped and peered round to see if Brown or Smith were there.

Two large women were standing on the pavement chatting to each other and masking his view of the car. One of the women had a pushchair with a small boy sitting in it. He took a bright red lollipop out of his mouth, wiped it down her cream skirt, then put it back in his mouth. After a few more licks, he repeated the operation.

Angel pulled out his mobile and scrolled down to a number and clicked on it.

It was soon answered.

'Yes, sir?' It was DS Carter.

'I urgently need backup, Flora,' he said. He quickly told her the situation and his requirements. She replied positively and then he ended the call.

He peered round the corner and was pleased to find the two women had moved a few metres away so that he now had an unrestricted view of the car.

And then Angel saw him.

Ezra Brown, as big and smart as a mannequin in the window of a plus-size clothing store. He was standing by the driver's door of the big car, gazing round, presumably for Moss. His face looked as if he had expected to be in a florist's but discovered he was in a fishmonger's instead.

Angel's skin tingled.

Then suddenly, Angel felt a tap on his shoulder. He turned and received a mighty blow on the chin from Reg Smith, who had silently crept up behind him.

Smith landed a second blow to his chin with his left fist. Angel lost daylight for a moment.

Then Angel's instinct took over as he grabbed Smith by his lapels and delivered a powerful uppercut, then another, then a third. Then he released his grip. Smith slithered to the ground. Angel stood back, panting, looking at his opponent and waiting for him to stand up.

Smith soon recovered and stood up, and Angel socked him on the chin. His teeth rattled. Smith quickly retaliated with a sharp jab to Angel's stomach which caused him to bend forward. Smith anticipated the reaction and caught Angel on the chin. They were powerful punches. Angel went down but soon sprang back. He grabbed Smith's lapels again and dealt him three massive slugs to the chin then pushed him away. Smith staggered two steps then fell heavily backwards on to the ground.

Angel ran a hand through his hair to push it back. Then he went across to the crook and looked down at him.

Smith's eyes were closed. He was breathing heavily.

Angel rolled Smith on to his face. He crouched down and pulled Smith's arms and wrists together at his back, then reached into his pocket for the handcuffs.

He was stopped when he heard a commanding voice say, 'Angel, if you pull a gun out of your pocket you're a dead pigeon.'

Angel looked up. Ezra Brown was standing at the top of the path at the corner of the theatre with his feet apart, pointing a gun at him.

All the muscles in Angel's body tightened.

He stood up.

Then he slowly took his hand out of his pocket, stretched his fingers and showed both sides, like a conjuror would before a trick.

'Don't expect applause, Angel,' Brown said. 'Just watch what you're doing, or I might have to shoot your hand off.'

Angel noticed how Brown's eyes seemed to glow frighteningly when he was under pressure.

Suddenly Smith groaned and rolled over. He opened his eyes and felt his chin, then stood up and saw Brown. He blinked.

Brown looked at him expressionlessly.

Smith's face creased up. 'I was just getting on top of him when he put on some knuckle-dusters. I hadn't a chance.'

'Put a squib up that AA man's arse and tell him I need my car *straightaway*,' Brown said. 'And see if you can see anything of Moss—'

'Moss?' Smith asked.

Brown, suddenly angry, pulled back his lips, baring his teeth. 'Yes, Moss!' he screamed. 'He should have been waiting for me at the car. Am I surrounded by idiots?'

Smith hurried round the corner on to the busy shopping street.

Then Brown said, 'Angel, move yourself over to that wall where I can see you. And put your hands up.'

Angel did as he was instructed. He hoped he wasn't about to be shot.

'I sent you a present recently,' Brown said. 'With a message. I assume you received it.'

'If you mean the brick through the window, Brown — oh yes, I received it, all right.'

'Why have you totally ignored the message attached?'

'It was the way it was delivered. No card. No chocolates or flowers. No invitation to dinner. And you didn't even say please.'

'And you're prepared to die for your principles?'

'I don't spend time worrying about principles. I hope to have a long and happy life. And I don't expect to die until I'm old and grey.'

'Well, what would you think if I told you that you're about to die in the next few minutes?'

Angel's stomach turned over and bounced. His heartbeat raced. He thought he wouldn't be able to speak, but he took hold of himself. 'For that you would be caught and punished. The force never give up looking for a man who's killed one of their own, and the judiciary would never award a light sentence to a cop killer. You would never taste the luxury of freedom again.'

Brown was silent for a few moments. 'How does ten thousand pounds sound to you?'

'Sounds great. But if you're trying to bribe me, you can forget it.'

'What about twenty-five thousand pounds?'

Angel dithered slightly as these sums were offered to him. With that sort of money, he could clear his and Mary's credit cards, pay off their mortgage and still have money for holidays. He had heard how great it was to go to the Maldives and other exotic places.

'No chance,' Angel said.

'Forty thousand pounds. That's the best I can do, Angel. Don't dismiss it lightly.'

'Forget it, Brown. You're wasting your breath.'

'With you on our side, we could clean up Bromersley and move on to Wakefield, then Leeds. We could easily gross fifteen thousand a week. Your share would be five thousand pounds a week . . . not just for one week, every week.'

Angel knew that he wouldn't be able to look in the mirror again. He wouldn't be able to look at Mary. He wouldn't be able to walk down the street with a warrant card in his pocket.

'No thank you,' Angel said.

Brown swallowed. He was about to speak but stopped.

Above the usual high street noise they heard the familiar two-tone siren of an emergency vehicle getting louder and louder.

Brown's eyes moved quickly to the left, then back.

Angel felt relieved. He closed his eyes briefly and smiled.

Smith appeared at the top of the path and whispered something to Brown. Brown didn't look pleased. He whispered something back and Smith ran off.

Brown said, 'Angel, I've given you every chance. Turn round. Face the wall.'

A rat with cold feet ran down Angel's spine. His stomach turned over. Should he face his killer? He *was* armed. He had two guns on him, but he wouldn't have time to pull them out of his pocket. And he didn't feel that brave.

Should he say a prayer? 'Oh Lord God, have mercy on me,' he mouthed. 'O Lord, look after my darling Mary. Keep her safe.' His stomach was churning. His thoughts were all over the place. *Oh my God, is he going to shoot? Is he ever going to pull that trigger?*

Suddenly he dropped his arms and pulled the Beretta out of his jacket pocket, whipped round at great speed, dived to the ground, rolled over twice, then held up his gun looking for Brown.

There was no Brown. There was nobody. Brown had gone.

Angel raced up the path to the main road. He looked around. Neither Brown nor Smith nor their car were to be seen.

A police patrol car glided up to Helliwell's fish shop with its engine running. Its emergency lights were still flashing but its siren was silent. In the driver's seat was PC Donohue.

Angel rushed up to him. 'Sean, have you seen that big black car on the move . . . the one you demobilised?'

'No, sir. But I've only just got here. Got a general call from DS Carter that you needed assistance. I was near. So here I am.'

Angel considered sending Donohue out to look for the villains, but taking into account that neither the patrolman nor himself had the slightest clue which direction they might have taken, he decided against it.

'Thank you, Sean. Have a look around the town, and if you see anything give me a ring.'

'Right, sir,' he said and drove away.

Almost immediately, DS Carter arrived in her unmarked car. At her side was DC Scrivens.

'You're about two minutes too late, Flora,' Angel said. 'The birds have flown again.'

Carter said, 'I couldn't have been any sooner, sir.'

'All is not lost, Flora. I have a prisoner: Moss. *And* his gun.'

Angel dug into his pocket and gave her the old Smith & Wesson through her car window. 'Hand it in when you get to the station, will you, Flora? I'll do the paperwork later.'

She took the gun and put it in her shoulder bag in the car.

'Where's Moss?' she said.

'In my car. He's cuffed, but I want Scrivens to sit in the back with him. Come on Ted . . . let's get him back to the station.'

THIRTEEN

Half an hour later, DI Angel, DS Carter, the duty officer Sergeant Clifton and the prisoner Moss were in the charge room at Bromersley Police Station.

Clifton looked at the prisoner. 'Sigmund Moss, you are being arrested for being in possession of an unlicensed firearm with the intention of aiding and abetting others to commit crimes of extortion. Your arrest is necessary to allow the prompt and effective investigation of the offence and to prevent further offences taking place. You do not have to say anything, but it may harm your defence if you do not mention when questioned something which you later rely on in court, and anything you do say may be given in evidence. Do you understand that?'

'Yes,' Moss said. 'And I want to see a brief. A good 'un.'

'The duty solicitor is Mr Bloom,' Clifton said. 'Unless you already have a solicitor, I'll give him a ring.'

'Righto, so no more questions until I've seen him. Will somebody take these effing bracelets off?'

Angel said, 'Bernie, I'll leave him with you.'

'Right, sir. What about visitors?'

'Just his legal team, and close family.'

'Right, sir.'

Angel turned away but then turned back. 'And, Bernie,' he said in a quiet voice, 'he's a bit stroppy and has a lot to say. Give him a quiet life for a few hours.'

Clifton nodded knowingly. 'Then he'll be bursting at the seams to talk.'

'Let's hope so, Bernie. Let's hope so. Come on, Flora. We must get to the convent. Let's see if the searches have revealed anything.'

* * *

The three surviving sisters, Precious, Clare and Emma, and the three women police officers were in the sitting room. Precious was reading. Clare and Emma were embroidering a white altar cloth. The three women police officers were busy writing.

Angel said, 'Stay here, Flora. I'll go and find Don Taylor.'

Taylor was in the Reverend Mother's office.

'Did you find anything interesting in the body searches, Don?'

'They're still writing out their reports, sir,' Taylor said. 'But both Sister Emma and Sister Clare have separately asked to see you urgently, sir. Neither of them would tell me what it was about.'

Angel lowered his eyebrows. 'Send one of them in and leave us on our own, will you, Don?'

'Right, sir,' he said and rushed off.

Angel sat at the desk which the Reverend Mother had not long since occupied. He looked round the little room at the crosses, crucifixes and prints of Jesus and the saints that covered the plain white walls. Angel found it very atmospheric, and he wondered how many earnest prayers had been said by good people inside those clean, white walls.

There was a gentle knock on the door. It was Sister Emma, carrying her missal. She gripped it very tightly and held it across her chest.

'Come in, Sister,' Angel said with a welcoming smile. 'You wanted to see me urgently? Please sit down.'

She smiled thinly. 'Yes. Thank you, Inspector.'

'Now, what did you want to see me about?'

Emma turned to look back at the door then looked back at Angel, as if she now regretted coming.

'Erm . . . yes, Inspector. It's in the way of a statement . . . a confession.'

Angel blinked. 'A confession? Do you mind if I record this, Sister?'

'Oh, yes. All right.'

He took a small recorder out of his top pocket, switched it on to record and put it on the desk between them.

Emma looked at it but said nothing.

He pointed at the recorder on the desk. 'You will have to speak.'

'Oh? Yes. Erm . . .'

Angel thought she had lost the thread of what she wanted to say.

Eventually she swallowed and said, 'Well, I have not been telling the truth . . . the exact truth about . . . Well, the fact is, I murdered Sister Julia, Sister Teresa and Father Morgan.'

Angel was dumbfounded.

'I could not stand the way they all kept telling me what to do,' she said. 'I was never really treated as an adult. As you will know from my records, my mother was a sister here before leaving the order to have me, but throughout everything, she never lost her strong faith in God. And it was my dear mother's faith that influenced me to become a nun. But she was more tolerant that I could ever be. Oh, I have a strong Christian faith too, but I don't accept all the teachings and some of the stupid traditions and beliefs that the Church hierarchy has inflicted upon its servants in the name of Jesus. I am one of the lowest of His servants, but I still have a right to an opinion and a voice.' She paused then said, 'Well, there it is. May the Lord have mercy upon me.'

Angel wiped his face with his hand, looked at her and eventually said, 'Before you go any further, Sister, I must advise you to get a solicitor to represent you.'

'I don't want or need anyone to tell me what to say.'

'It's not only that, Emma. A solicitor knows the ropes and is the way towards getting a barrister to represent you in high court, where you will be tried.'

'There's no need for all that. I'm guilty. As a bride of Christ, I have promised to love everybody, but I can't. Just punish me. Send me to prison. I have broken a commandment three times.'

Angel looked down at the polished desktop and sighed. He rubbed his temples.

By rights he should charge Sister Emma with murder and lock her up. From that moment on, had she been allowed to go free, he would indirectly be responsible should any harm come to anyone else, and he would have his conscience to live with. A decision would have to be made and it would have to be made there and then.

'I hope you know what you're doing, Sister.'

'I certainly do, Inspector.'

Angel reached over to the recorder, stopped it. Then he took out his phone and rang DS Carter.

'Flora, come along into the Reverend Mother's office. I want you to witness Sister Emma being arrested.'

* * *

'Sit down, Sister,' Angel said. 'And what did you urgently want to see me about?'

'Thank you, Inspector,' Clare said, 'and I'll come straight to the point. It seems very possible that there is a danger of you arresting the wrong person for the murders of Father Morgan, and my sisters, Julia and Teresa. I believe that you think Sister Precious is the guilty one. But it is not so. Charging her with the murders would be so unjust. She has served her time as a sister faithfully and justly for fifty years or more. I know that she is crusty sometimes. And a stickler for procedure and so on. But she has earned her crown. And she has notified Bishop Letterman of the murder of Sister Teresa, and she has been in touch with the Mother Superior of our order in Northumberland, who is sending four seasoned sisters and two novices here to take over the responsibilities of the convent and maintain the tradition and security of the finger of Saint Ethel. So I can absolutely assure you that she is innocent of these killings. I know this with such certainty because I murdered all three, and I am ready to serve my worldly punishment.'

Angel looked at her and sighed.

* * *

'Yes, sir,' the frustrated PC said into the phone. 'I understand that the two nuns must be kept apart, but how can I do that when we don't have any patrol cars to spare? Most of the force is out looking for the insurance racketeers.'

'Then send two of them — Brown and Smith have both been to the convent before. The drivers can keep an eye out for them on the way over,' Angel said. 'It's not two miles from the convent to the station. Both suspects have been thoroughly searched. Neither of them has a submachine gun hidden under their habit.'

Angel ended the call, screwed up his face angrily and shoved the phone into his pocket.

Carter came into the Reverend Mother's office carrying some papers in a fawn folder. She put it on the desk in front of him. 'The report on the body searches of the three sisters,' she said.

'Ah yes,' he said eagerly. 'Thank you.'

She went out.

At a glance he could see that there was nothing of interest from the police officers who had searched Precious and

Clare, just a short simple paragraph each, but the one who examined Emma had written:

While the suspect has a head of thinly spread healthy-looking hair, in two patches, she was bald. Sister Emma said she had seen the doctor and he had prescribed some ointment, but she said that it didn't seem to be much good. She said the problem had started in her teens. It grows and dies when and where it likes. She went on to say that, as she belonged to an order that did not permit her to show her hair, the hair loss did not inconvenience her in any way.

Angel rubbed his chin.

His mobile rang.

'Angel,' he said.

It was DC Scrivens.

'What is it, Ted?'

'I thought you'd want to know that Ruth Levi died early this morning in the General Hospital, sir. It was on local radio. Her family were with her. It said she had seventy-per-cent burns and never fully recovered from the fire in the antiques shop on Friday night.'

'Oh,' Angel gasped.

That was a terrible blow. He'd liked Ruth — she had seemed to him a loving, caring woman with everything to live for.

'Right, Ted.'

He ended the call and closed his eyes briefly. He stood up. He knew exactly where he had to be.

He went downstairs to the sitting room, where the two prisoners were seated with Carter.

Carter stood up and came over to him. 'What's happening, sir?'

Quietly he said, 'I'm going out. HQ is sending over a couple of cars to pick up the prisoners.' He looked from one nun to the other. 'Keep your eye on Sister Emma and Sister

Clare. I don't want them communicating with each other. One of them is a liar.'

'I know. I know. And the other is a murderer.'

'Ring me on my mobile if you need me.'

He reached his car, started the engine and pointed it at the hospital. He didn't want to go, but at this time, it was the only place to be.

* * *

Angel was in time to take Mr Levi and his mother-in-law in his car from the General Hospital to her home in an estate on the perimeter of town. As Ruth's mother collected her two granddaughters from a neighbour, Levi made a pot of tea.

Angel did his best to ease forward the necessary business of a family in mourning and managed to assist them to get the necessary death certificate and engage an undertaker. A few tears were shed, but all in all they were a very brave family.

Angel's phone rang.

It was Scrivens again. 'Sorry to bother you, sir, but the super is screaming out for you.'

'Right, Ted. I'll come in straightaway.'

Angel took his leave courteously from the Levi family.

'Thank you, Inspector,' Mr Levi said. 'We are most grateful for your presence, companionship and support.'

It warmed Angel's heart. He smiled and said, 'I'll see you again soon.'

* * *

'Well, sit down, Angel,' Harker snapped when he arrived in his superior's office. 'There. Opposite me. Where I can see you.'

Angel sat down on the only chair his side of the desk.

'I expect you know why I've sent for you.'

'No sir. I have no idea.'

Harker sighed impatiently. 'I suppose you think this place is the Dorchester Hotel, and that we're short of residents.'

'No, sir. I don't. I suppose you're referring to the arrests of Moss, and the two nuns from the convent?'

'Indeed I am. Who is this Sigmund Moss?'

'I've charged him with being in possession of a deadly weapon. He's the one who shot at me outside the Bull at Cropstitch when I was trying to arrest Brown. But he's also driver, bag carrier and general dogsbody to Brown. We should be able to charge him with a lot more.'

Harker said, 'Well, get him on the magistrates' list tomorrow. Move him on quickly.' He looked down at his notes, then looked up. 'Now, whoever has heard of the arrest of two nuns for . . . for . . . anything?'

'Both of them have *confessed* to the murder of the priest and two sisters, sir. What else could I do?'

'They were in it together, eh?'

'They both say they executed all three murders entirely on their own. Obviously this can't be true of both of them.'

'Well, then, you should release them both until you find the truth.'

'If I do that, sir, I'm potentially allowing the guilty one to fly the coop. I can't do that.'

Harker shook his head irritably. 'Well, you shouldn't have arrested them both until you knew which one was the guilty one.'

Angel lost his patience. 'But they *confessed*, sir,' he exclaimed. 'Both of them *confessed*. Within minutes of each other. What else was I to do?'

'Don't you raise your voice at me!'

'It's not safe to let the murderer go free. She's murdered three people. If she gets away she could murder another . . . or even more.'

'All right. All right. But the problem is the expense of providing five-star accommodation for three prisoners. Three meals a day. And I also have to provide — out of an already depleted staff — a jailor twenty-four-seven. And if you have two confessions to the same murder, a defence barrister would make mincemeat of the CPO if it came to crown court. You *must* determine which woman is the murderer. Then charge the other with wasting police time.'

Angel wasn't pleased. He had to admit that Harker had a valid point. He came out of the office with a face like thunder. He saw a paper cup on the floor by the drinks machine and kicked it with all his might towards his own office. It needed two more equally violent kicks to get it all the way back to his office door, where he picked it up and dropped it in his waste bin.

He sat at his desk, and from the pile of reports, letters and general bumf, he pulled out the statements made by Clare and Emma immediately after the murder of the priest, as well as the statements taken from them after each of the murders of the two nuns. He read them all and then sat back in the swivel chair for a brief moment. Then he rang DS Carter and DC Scrivens and asked them to join him.

He told them both about the meeting he had had with the superintendent and then said, 'It's strange. I have a problem I've never had in a case before. One of two sisters is guilty of murder, but instead of having to find out who is guilty, I have to find out who is innocent, so that by default the other must be the murderer.'

They both nodded thoughtfully.

'OK. Let's give it a try.'

He quickly outlined his plan to them and then said, 'Who shall we test first?'

Scrivens shrugged. 'Does it matter, sir?'

'Not at all,' he said. Then he added, 'Why don't we let providence play a hand?' He fumbled in his pocket and pulled out a one-pound piece. 'Let's toss a coin? Heads it's Clare, tails it's Emma.'

He flicked the coin in the air, caught it, slapped it on the back of his hand and revealed it first to Carter and then to Scrivens.

'Heads,' he said. 'So it's Sister Clare first. You two bring Clare and Emma to the convent. They must be kept separate at all times, so you will have to bring both of your cars. Handcuff them at the front and don't take any chances. Be at the convent in fifteen minutes.'

He pulled open his middle desk drawer and took out a paperknife. It was about the same weight and size of the stiletto. Then he looked around for something to simulate the holster. He couldn't hope to simulate the texture of leather, but he managed to approximate the bulk and weight with cardboard retrieved from his waste bin wrapped round the paperknife and secured with sticky tape.

He put the model in his pocket, went out to his car and made for the convent ahead of the others. He rang the bell.

The door was eventually answered by little Sister Precious, who was wearing a kitchen apron over her usual habit.

'Oh, it's you, Inspector Angel,' she said in very small voice. 'Please come in.'

He went into the hall.

'Sister Precious. Are you managing on your own satisfactorily?'

'Oh, yes. But I'm glad you're here — it's nice not to be alone.'

He closed the door. 'I've come to do some tests with Sister Emma and Sister Clare. Are you still occupying the bedroom named after Saint Peter?'

'No. I'm not superstitious or anything like that, but I didn't like staying there any longer. Not at a time when the convent — a house of God — is experiencing such evil. I moved to Saint John's, two rooms away. And how are my two dear sisters?'

'They're doing very well, apparently . . . I'm bringing them here soon, and I'll be using Saint Peter's and your sitting room for a short time. I would ask you not to visit those rooms for a little while and not to speak to either of them if you see them. In fact, it would be better if you were not seen by them at all.'

Precious's face went scarlet. 'Not seen!' she said. 'What? I may not look at my own dear sisters . . . in my . . . in *their* own home? Very well. I will stay in the kitchen. I was in the middle of preparing my lunch when you rang the bell.'

She began to walk away, grinding her teeth and muttering, 'I will stay in the kitchen where I belong . . . I know my place . . . Bless my dear sisters, oh Lord, and please help me to remain humble . . .'

She turned left at the end of the hall and made her way to the kitchen.

'I'll answer the doorbell when it rings, Sister,' he called.

He wasn't pleased to have upset her. He wondered if he could have worded his request differently. She had gone off in a huff, and he couldn't even apologise or explain. He had to drop it . . . there was no other way . . . forget it. Oh dear.

Through the hall window, he saw Carter with Sister Clare in handcuffs making for the front door. He hurried down the hall to the door and opened it to avoid them ringing the bell and possibly further frustrating Sister Precious.

They followed him upstairs to the room known as Saint Peter's.

Angel stopped them outside the door.

He turned to Carter. 'Take the cuffs off.'

Then he went into the room to check that the picture of Saint Peter was hanging on the wall from a high position opposite the bed as before, and that no additional furniture had been added to the room, like a stool or a chair.

There was a rattle of keys as Carter unlocked the handcuffs.

Clare sighed with relief and rubbed her chafed wrists.

Angel came out of the room on to the landing. He showed the simulated stiletto in a leather holster he had contrived from a paperknife and cardboard to Clare.

He explained what it was supposed to be. 'I am well aware that you know *where* the stiletto was concealed. What I would like to know is how you managed to hide it there.'

Then he held out the cardboard-covered paperknife to her. 'Will you take this model and show me?'

Sister Clare looked at him and frowned. 'Is that all you want me to do?'

Angel nodded. 'That's all.'

Clare took the model, nodded and looked at the door.

He turned to Carter. 'Will you video this business, Flora?'

Carter took out her phone and set it up.

Angel indicated with a gesture that Carter should go into the room first.

She took up a position in the corner of the room.

Angel looked at Clare. 'Whenever you're ready, Sister. I'll follow you in.'

Clare nodded and walked through the open door.

Angel followed with a stopwatch in his hand.

Without looking round the little room, Sister Clare took hold of the bed by the rail at the bottom and pushed it about a metre so that it was directly under the picture of Saint Peter. Then she slipped off her sandals, stood up on the end of the bed in her stockinged feet, dropped the model down the back of the picture, then came down off the bed, pushed it back into position and put on her sandals.

The whole business took twenty-six seconds.

'Was that all right, Inspector?'

'Absolutely. Thank you.'

Angel and Carter exchanged glances.

'Put the cuffs back on, Carter,' Angel said.

Clare pulled a face. 'Are they really necessary?'

'I'm afraid so,' Angel said, as he reached up the wall to retrieve the model. He managed to lift the bottom edge of the picture frame with his fingertips and the model dropped into his hand. He put it back in his pocket.

Carter held the handcuffs out to Sister Clare. 'If you had been a man, you would have had them fastened at the back, which is much worse.'

Clare resignedly held out her wrists.

Carter fitted them on her in a couple of seconds, then led her downstairs. For reasons of security, Angel followed them all the way to Carter's car outside the convent gate.

Angel saw them off then returned to the convent. He went into the sitting room, where Sister Emma and DC Scrivens were waiting to be called.

They followed Angel up a flight of stairs to Saint Peter's.

Angel said, 'When the time comes, will you video this on your phone?'

'Yes, sir, of course,' Scrivens said.

Angel repeated to Emma the instructions word for word he had delivered to Clare, and when it came to putting the model behind the picture, Emma, being very tall, simply reached up, pulled the picture away from the wall with one hand and with the other tucked the model under the frame, then put the frame back in position, and it was done.

Angel timed it. It took twelve seconds.

FOURTEEN

Angel was at his desk back at the station. He looked as if he was changing a dirty nappy.

Carter sat at the other side of his desk. 'What's the matter, sir?'

· 'I expected that at least one of them would have difficulty in replacing the stiletto under the picture. But it didn't faze either of them. Emma seemed to know that she was tall enough to easily reach the picture and unhesitatingly went straight to it. Clare pulled and pushed the bed with the greatest of ease . . . as if she did it every day. I don't think I've learned anything.'

'Perhaps you underestimated their intelligence?'

'Not at all. It would have been more intelligent for one of them to *pretend* that they found it difficult to put the stiletto behind the picture.'

'Like Sister Precious?' Carter said.

Angel rubbed his chin. The lines on his forehead turned to deeper wrinkles.

'I don't know if she pretended . . .'

He reminded himself that the convent was sealed up that night, so the murderer of Sister Teresa had to be either Sister Emma, Sister Clare or Sister Precious.

He reached for the phone and tapped in DS Taylor's number.

'Don, any news on the forensics for Sister Teresa's body?'

'The samples have gone to the lab, sir. It'll take a week or so.'

'I know that. But you've had preliminary results, surely — you've had a sneaky look, haven't you?'

'There were no hairs found, but at a glance the samples taken appeared to be pretty much of the same composition as those from the other two victims. By the way, you'll want to see the contents of Sigmund Moss's pockets. I'll send those up, with the inventory.'

'Oh, yes. Thank you.'

'The custody sergeant told me earlier that Moss keeps calling out that he's being ignored by everybody and that he should be interviewed.'

Angel gave a satisfied sigh. 'I know, Don. I know.'

'What did he say, sir?' Carter asked once Angel had hung up.

'He said that the samples looked pretty much the same as was found on Richard Morgan and the Reverend Mother . . . their own skin, beeswax, charcoal and resin.'

Carter said, 'I can understand the beeswax and the charcoal, but the resin leaves me guessing.'

'Leaves me guessing too, Flora,' he said. 'I must contact Bishop Letterman and see if he can throw any more light on the situation.'

There was a knock on the door and Sergeant Mallin put his head through the gap. 'Am I intruding, sir?'

Angel said, 'Is my car ready, Norman?'

Sergeant Norman Mallin was in charge of the police station's transport.

'Yes, sir. It was only the replacement of the windscreen, wasn't it?'

'Yes.'

'Here are the keys. It's parked out front. I've had it washed, waxed and polished. Good as new.'

Angel smiled. 'Thank you, Norman.'

Mallin went out and closed the door.

Angel looked at Carter. 'Right, let's take a look at what was in Moss's pockets. There must be something that will lead us to Mr Ezra Brown.'

Carter passed him a letter tray with a large polythene bag containing Sigmund Moss's personal effects with an inventory on a sheet of A4 stuck to it with sticky tape.

Angel looked down the inventory. He spotted 'Driving Licence' on the list. He emptied the polythene bag into the tray and fished around for Moss's licence. It was in a wallet with money and other items. The address on the card was given as Vesty's Lodge, Vesty's Lane, Tressingham, Huddersfield. That was no help. He'd already been there and Brown's gang had left in a hurry. He rooted through the wallet. There was money, a points card with Cheapo's Supermarket and a receipt.

Angel smiled and waved the paper at Carter. 'I think we may have something, Flora. This is a receipt for eighty pounds from the Bromersley Heating and Lighting Centre, Queen Street, for a paraffin heater to be delivered on this Saturday morning just gone.'

Carter smiled and held out her hand. He gave it to her.

'Why would he want a paraffin heater?' she said.

'I don't know. Go and find out. And find out the address it had to be delivered to, that's what I want to know.'

She stood up. 'I'll do what I can, sir.'

'Don't mention that you're police. That information might well be passed on to Brown. Could you pretend to be someone else?'

* * *

DS Carter stopped outside the Bromersley Heating and Lighting Centre on Queen Street and went into the shop. It was a big shop with lots of gas and electric fires on show. There were two customers with salesmen discussing possible purchases.

Carter made directly for a young man behind a long counter at the far end of the shop floor.

She took the receipt out of her handbag, and, assuming a brisk and sharp manner, said, 'Excuse me, is this one of your receipts?'

'Erm. It appears to be. Yes, madam.'

'It's incorrect. It says delivery on Saturday morning, twenty-sixth of November.'

'Yes it does. Was it not delivered?'

'No it wasn't.'

'I'm very sorry. One moment, please. I'll look at the delivery log.'

He turned to a computer on the countertop and tapped in a few details. After a few seconds he frowned and said, 'I don't understand that, madam. It was on the van for delivery on Saturday and it was signed for by . . . I *think* it says "S. Wass".'

'May I see?'

He turned the screen round for Carter to see. The signature was 'S. Moss'.

'Where was it delivered to?'

He tapped another key. 'Top floor, Duxbury Mill, Top Bobbin Hill, Bromersley.'

Carter was surprised and elated but she didn't show it. Instead, she discarded the brisk attitude. 'Oh, I see,' she said. 'That explains it. Sorry to have troubled you.'

'That's all right, madam. Have a nice day.'

* * *

Angel rubbed his chin and repeated what Carter had just said. 'Duxbury Mill?'

'That's what he said.'

'Well, it's a huge, stark, very old building. Top floor. That's up eight levels. That's a lot of shoe leather. If somebody's spending time up there they *will* find it cold in November. I went through the building a few years ago . . . looking for an escapee from Armley.'

'Did you find him?'

'No. Is it possible that Brown and Smith are hiding out up there?'

'Mr Diamond occupies the ground floor doesn't he?' Carter said. 'He'll probably know what's happening up there. We can ask *him*.'

Angel pursed his lips and shook his head. 'No. We don't know what's going on. We don't know their relationship. Let's keep this information secret. In the past we may have trusted too many people. This time let's keep absolutely schtum.'

Carter nodded. 'Right, sir. What *are* you going to do?'

'I don't know, Flora. I'm thinking about it.'

He passed her the paper tray containing Moss's possessions. 'I don't think there's anything else useful to us in there. Will you see that the SOCOs get it back? Maybe it's time to talk to Mr Sigmund Moss.'

* * *

The duty jailer let Angel into Moss's cell then locked the door. Moss was lounging on his bed but stood up when he saw Angel.

They looked each other over and Angel said, 'Now then, Moss, what's all the fuss about? What do you want?'

'You're Detective Inspector Angel, aren't you?' Moss said. 'And you have a wife called Mary.'

Angel's body stiffened when he heard Mary's name. He was always concerned for her safety. How did Moss know her name? And why did he mention it? He was glad that she was safely away in Scotland.

Moss sniffed. 'I've been here all day and I haven't seen anybody.'

'Have you seen your solicitor?'

'Yes, of course. I mean I haven't been interviewed.'

'You know full well that you're charged with possession of a firearm,' Angel said. 'That's what we're holding you with. But there are many charges to follow . . . from the day you first joined Ezra Brown and began to assist him in his extortion racket in Bromersley right up to when I catch him and Smith at their last caper in Duxbury Mill.'

Moss froze and his eyes flashed when he heard Angel mention Duxbury Mill. He clenched his fists.

Angel said, 'Anyway, what have you been calling out for? Was it to tell me something useful . . . something I don't already know?'

'Fat chance of that,' Moss said.

'I'm surprised at you being so cocky. Now that your career as a bully boy is over, I thought you might have shown some sense and helped us to put Brown and Smith in the dock. If you were to assist us now, I can say that the judge would be told and it may lighten your sentence.'

'I'm no copper's nark, Angel. I'll take my chances.'

'Who's the next person or business he's going to put the squeeze on?'

Moss breathed in deeply and looked at Angel. Then he breathed out slowly, looked away and shook his head. 'No comment.'

'What is Brown's interest in Duxbury Mill?'

* * *

It was 8.30 the following morning, Tuesday, 29 November. Angel was at the convent door.

Sister Precious opened the door. 'Oh, it's you, Inspector. Please come in.'

Angel smiled and walked into the hall. 'Are you managing all right on your own, Sister?'

'Oh yes, very well, thank you.'

'I would prefer you had some company, Sister Precious. At least until we get this murderer caught and put away. And you shouldn't be alone with only one other person, unless you know that person very, very well indeed.'

'I don't fear death, Inspector. Don't worry on my account. I'm never completely on my own. My heavenly Father is never far away. And there's a lot to do here to keep everything clean and safe, observe my offices and look after myself. And for other matters, I always have Bishop Letterman to refer to.'

'If there was an emergency, does he have access to the convent?'

'Oh yes. He has a full set of keys to the convent as well as our chapel.'

Angel nodded. 'Good,' he said.

Angel needed to see Bishop Letterman in the very near future. It was very important. He must remember to phone him.

'When are the new members of your community arriving?' he said.

'Bishop Letterman said a week or so. I expect them anytime now. I want everything spotless and in order when they arrive. Come into the office. Sit down.'

'Thank you, Sister.'

'Now, you didn't come here to ask how I was doing, Inspector, did you?'

'To tell the truth, I came to ask you about Duxbury Mill. I understand that the convent owns it?'

'Oh, yes. Mr Diamond is our tenant. He's a lovely man, Inspector. The good Lord blesses us with good fortune.'

Angel leaned over the desk. 'Now, I want to ask you a question, Sister, and I want you to treat it in absolute confidence.'

'I can do that, Inspector. As a religious person, I will take a great many secrets with me to Paradise, when the good Lord calls me.'

'I'm sure you will. Have you made any arrangement recently with any other person or company to look round Duxbury Mill, execute repairs or rent it from you, or to be present in the place for any reason at all?'

'No. I only wish we could. We could do with the income. Why? Have you seen some activity?'

'No. I haven't seen anything, Sister.'

'Not surprising,' she said. 'It's all locked up. Mr Diamond rents the ground floor, and access to the other seven floors is secured by a thick steel door with a big lock. The entrance to the top floors is independent from the entrance to the ground floor.'

'I need to look round the building, Sister. Who has the key?'

'The key is here in this desk, or it was when I was Reverend Mother. Mr Diamond would probably know if somebody is around. You could ask him.'

'No, Sister. I want to keep the police's interest in the building absolutely secret. If there are any intruders there, we want to catch them, not chase them away. But I would like to have the key and have a look round.'

Sister Precious pulled open the middle drawer and ferreted around among stationery, pens, pencils and keys. 'It was here with a label attached to it, if I remember correctly . . . ah, here it is.'

She handed him a large old black key with a brown label swinging from it. Angel looked at the label. It read: 'Duxbury Mill'.

* * *

It was 5.45 p.m. that same day when Angel drove his BMW into the garage, doused the lights, locked the car and pulled down the garage door. After a quick meal of beans on toast, he patted his jacket pockets to check he had the Beretta Tomcat in one and the Duxbury Mill key in the other. Then he put on an overcoat and hat, picked up his night-time binoculars from the old hall stand and went out back to the car. He drove it out of the garage and pulled down the overhead door.

It was very cold. His breath made clouds in the clear moonlight.

While Duxbury Mill was on the rising slope of a hill, there was another rise about two hundred metres away which was a small woodland area popular with bird watchers and walkers.

Angel parked his car on the rise among several evergreen trees, facing the huge eight-storey stone building with dozens of black windows and an enormous sign with the single word 'DUXBURY' painted on it in white.

He doused the lights and the ignition, then took out his binoculars and focused them on the windows of the building.

Diamond's business had closed down for the night so the mill was in total darkness.

Angel moved methodically from window to window hoping to see some light or activity, particularly on the top floor. There was nothing. He continued peering through the lenses until his eyes were tired and he was seeing double. At length, he lowered the binoculars, blinked and looked at his watch. It was ten o'clock. He pursed his lips in thought . . .

If Ezra Brown and Reg Smith *were* in the building, he would have expected to see some activity by now. However, if they were . . . apprehensive — and they ought to be — perhaps they quite sensibly were being very, very careful.

Angel resolved to stay on watch at least until after midnight.

His thoughts turned to Mary. She was returning home on Friday. He couldn't wait to have her back. He needed to get Brown and Smith enjoying the comfort of a private cell each in Bromersley Police Station before her return.

Mary could spot when he was worrying about something and she would find a comforting remark that allayed his fears. And when he or anybody else was pulling somebody to pieces, she would always find something good to say about the person.

He enjoyed her company best when it was just the two of them. He loved her presence, her love, her hair, her eyes, her warmth, her touch, her thighs . . .

His eyes were tired. He closed them.

He fell asleep.

About ninety minutes later he woke up shivering. He started the car and ran the heater. When he was comfortable again, he picked up the binoculars and looked out at the mill. The moon had moved round a few degrees and was now illuminating the back of the building more strongly. The two end windows on the top floor showed up a light colour, which could be cream or beige. Could that indicate blackout blinds of some sort? That might allow Brown and Smith to light the space after dark without being observed from outside. They could take the blackouts down during daylight hours.

Then he saw some movement he couldn't at first identify. Something was slowly travelling up the side of the massive building. It was an irregular shape. He realised it was a number of parcels in a string net, and hanging vertically above the net was something thin which shone occasionally as it caught the moonlight — a cable or rope. He remembered there was a simple hand-operated pulley on the top floor that swung out from the building, and would have once been used to transfer goods to and from the floors below.

The top floor and the floors directly below had doors that could be opened to the outside to receive and send raw materials, cloth or anything else. Somebody on the top floor must be winding a big wheel, which was slowly pulling the string net of irregular-shaped parcels and bags upwards. It could be shopping. It could be anything.

Angel watched the hoist eventually reach the top floor, when suddenly, he saw a man appear at the open door on the top floor. It *looked* like Ezra Brown. A great warmth spread through Angel's chest.

The man reached out with a long hook . . . he reached out to the rope and pulled the goods into the building. Shortly afterwards, he reappeared to close the doors. Angel had a longer and better view of the man.

It *was* Ezra Brown.

'Ah!' Angel said with delight. He lowered the binoculars and looked at his watch. It was a few minutes past midnight.

He wrinkled his face, checked the Beretta and transferred it to his overcoat pocket. Then he reversed the BMW out of the bushes and drove about a mile to a side street close to the mill. He didn't want to drive into the mill yard in case he was observed. He took a small torch and two sets of handcuffs off the dashboard shelf, put them in his pocket and locked the car. He walked quickly to the back of the mill and up to the big steel door. He unlocked it with the key, closed it, but didn't lock it. He flashed the torch around. There was another big steel door, which he reckoned would lead into the ground floor, Max Diamond's area. And there was a large set of stone steps leading upwards. It was around five metres wide and there was no handrail. He began to begin the trudge to the top. It was going to be a long and laborious plod. He stopped and rested when he reached the landing of the penultimate floor, and checked his access to his gun.

He took a deep breath and was about to head up the last staircase to the top floor when he flashed the torch downward and noticed a step that was different from the others. It was the same stone colour but had an even surface and a straight edge. On closer examination he saw that it was a plank of wood the length of the step and painted the same colour. He looked underneath it and saw a small pressure pad.

His jaw muscles tightened.

The principle was that when anyone put any weight on the plank, the pressure pad operated a switch that transmitted a signal to a device — possibly a firearm, though in this case more likely a buzzer, a bell or a warning light.

He gave that step a very wide berth.

As he reached the top-floor landing on tiptoe, he flashed his torch around. To the left was a massive empty floor space, broken by steel pillars that supported the roof. A few metres down the wall were the double doors which opened to the elements — this was where the hoist was located. The strong metal arm with the pulley was set high in the space. The big wheel with many metres of rope around it, which was manually operated, was to the right of the doors. There was a sign across the doors with red lettering: 'DANGER — KEEP AWAY FROM HOIST DOORS. Authorised staff only.'

To Angel's right were two wooden doors. In former days, one led to the foreman's office and the other to a storeroom.

There was a dim light showing beneath the door of the foreman's office.

Angel pocketed the torch and took hold of the door-knob. He turned it. It wasn't locked. He quickly pushed it wide open and walked in.

The illumination was from an oil lamp on a table between two iron-framed beds. He could see that only one bed was occupied. The occupant appeared to be fast asleep. Gun in hand, he cautiously approached the bed. He leaned over the sleeper. It was Ezra Brown.

It was then that he heard the rustle of clothes and felt a mighty blow to the back of his head. He dropped the Beretta and his eyes closed momentarily. He fell to the floor face downward and felt several kicks to his thigh and his side. He rolled over and saw his attacker. It was Smith. His face was red and twisted with anger. He attempted to kick Angel again but Angel caught his foot in both hands and sharply twisted it.

Smith screamed and yelled, 'Bastard!'

He fell to the floor with a loud bang.

Angel stood up and looked around for his Beretta. He couldn't see it anywhere.

Brown was now wide awake, standing on the bed in his pyjamas readying himself to leap on to Angel. Angel saw him coming just in time and moved quickly away so that Brown finished up on top of Smith, who had been getting up.

Angel pulled Brown off the top of Smith by his pyjama jacket collar and gave him a mighty punch on the jaw with his left fist. And another. And another.

Brown's head fell forward. He slumped down on to the floor. He was out for more than the conventional count.

Smith came towards Angel with clenched fists. Angel made several assaults on him but without success. Then

Smith delivered a powerful jab at Angel's chest, but Angel countered with a swing to the mouth. He followed this quickly with an uppercut to Smith's chin and a right to his jaw. Smith retaliated with a poorly aimed jab, which hit Angel's cheek, but he got a further smack to the chin for his trouble. Smith pulled back rubbing his jaw.

Although Angel was breathing heavily and perspiring, this was no time for rest. He advanced on Smith with his fists up. Smith, with his back literally against the wall, hit out at Angel and missed. Angel rained blow after blow on Smith. His left and then his right, each one more powerful than the last. Smith's eyes were half closed. His fists thrashed about aimlessly, not connecting with anything. Angel stopped the onslaught but kept up his guard.

Smith fell down. His head dropped. His eyes closed.

Angel, panting, crouched down and felt Smith's wrist. His pulse was strong and regular. Angel blew out a sigh. He quickly dug into his pocket and took out a pair of handcuffs. He snapped one cuff round Smith's wrist and the other round the L-shaped side of the iron bedframe.

He was satisfied that that would hold Smith secure.

In the process he saw where the Beretta gun had disappeared to. It was under Brown's bed but where Smith couldn't reach it.

'Stand up, Angel. And put your hands where I can see them.'

Angel spun round and found Brown was aiming a gun at him. While he had been securing Smith, Brown must have recovered and retrieved his Walther from wherever he had stashed it.

Angel wasn't ready to die. His stomach felt hollow and a shiver went down his spine.

'Put them up,' Brown said. 'Higher. Higher . . . that's it. I've got a plan for you. I have repeatedly told you to stop following us. But you seem to be deaf as well as stupid.'

Angel wrinkled his nose. 'And I have a plan for you. It involves thirteen honest people.'

'If that's your lucky number, I've got news for you: your luck ran out.'

'No. It's the judge and jury at the crown court.'

'You'll never get me to court.'

'Oh, yes I will.'

'This gun says you won't.'

'Even if you shoot me, the remainder of the force will take over and you'll go down for life.'

Brown's eyes bulged. His face went scarlet. He glared at Angel. 'Oh, I've had enough of this stupid talk.'

He pushed the gun forward. 'I've got a job for you. Keep your hands up, turn round and make for the door.'

Angel frowned, turned and walked slowly out of the room. His mind was everywhere. He knew Brown was desperate enough to kill him. As long as Brown held that gun he would have to do as he was told. If Brown wanted to shoot him, why not do it where they were? How would Mary manage? There was his police pension, but that wouldn't be enough . . .

'Turn right,' Brown said.

Angel turned right and stopped walking. He was facing the vast empty floor space and the forest of pillars.

'Right again. And keep walking.'

Angel was still thinking . . . Mary had never worked. How would she survive on his pension? She had no trade or profession.

He found himself facing the double doors of the hoist and the red warning sign. Realisation was beginning to dawn on him.

Oh no. He gasped. His heart came up to his mouth as he visualised himself dropping unsupported through the air, the wind rushing past and the hard tarmac coming up to meet him.

'I said keep walking,' Brown said.

Angel didn't move. His mind was in turmoil. He wasn't ready to die. There must be a way out.

'Keep walking, Angel.'

Angel hesitated then he went slowly across the red line and up to the hoist doors.

'Now, lift the security handle. Pull the door towards you.'

Angel saw a little notice on the doors that read: 'DANGER. Security handle. Lift to open. Down to lock.' He hesitated, but reached out to the handle and lifted it.

Brown nodded. 'Now, get hold of the handle of the door on the right, press it down and pull that door towards you.'

When Angel opened the door, the cold wind cut into his face and howled like the wail of a thousand bagpipes. When he glanced out he could see Bromersley's roads, and dots of light from some houses and illuminated large buildings — the hospital and the town hall. He looked down at the space immediately below. It was a dark void. His spine turned into an icicle.

'Now open the other door,' Brown said.

Angel looked at the way the left-hand door was opened. It was by two bolts. He pulled up the bolt from the bottom easily enough, but he pretended he couldn't move the bolt at the top of the door — anything to create a stay of execution.

'Don't fool around, Angel. Put some muscle into it.'

'It's stuck. It won't move,' he said, still pretending to struggle with it.

'I opened it myself an hour ago. It was easy.'

Angel looked at the non-existent soreness of his hands. 'It's no good. It needs hitting with something heavy to move it.'

Brown sighed heavily. He glared at Angel and stormed across the floor to the door. 'I'll do it,' he said. Then he pointed to the hoist wheel a metre away. 'Go over there and stand still. And remember, I'll be watching you every second.'

Angel had gained a short reprieve.

He took up the position and watched Brown closely.

Still pointing the Walther at the detective, Brown then went across to the open door, looked away for a second, pulled the bolt down and opened the other door.

In that second, Angel leapt from behind the hoist wheel and made a grab for the gun.

Brown pulled the trigger.

The bullet went downward, straight out through the floorboard.

Both men struggled by the open doors for possession of the gun. Angel brought up his knee into Brown's hip. It pushed Brown nearer the open doors. Angel then banged Brown's hand hard on the edge of the door three times. Brown yelled and dropped the gun. It bounced off Angel's shoe on to the floor, centimetres from the opening. They both bent forward to grab it, bumped into each other. Brown lost his balance, slipped and went over the edge. As he fell, he managed to hold by his fingertips the two-centimetre-high ridge on the floor where the doors abut when closed.

Angel dropped to his knees, pocketed the gun, grabbed hold of Brown's left wrist and tried to pull him up. He managed to hold him for a minute, and he tried to pull him up further but could not. He looked around.

'Hold on a minute!' he gasped.

Angel untangled Brown from his arm and left him holding on to the building by his fingertips.

'No,' Brown said. 'Don't leave me.'

'Only a few seconds. Hold on.'

Angel stood up and turned to the hoist. He released the holding brake, took the curved iron hook, pulled the rope two metres or so outside, lowered it to Brown's feet then put the brake on the hoist.

Brown yelled, 'I can't hold on any longer!'

'Just a few seconds.'

'For God's sake, Angel.'

Angel said, 'Put one foot in the hook. You'll have to feel for it. You can put your weight on it. And grip this rope. I'll have you inside in seconds.'

Brown found the hook, put his weight on it and gasped. Then he gripped the rope tightly and sighed with relief.

'I'm going to wind you in.'

Angel took the wheel and Brown slowly came up the side of the building and swung safely inside.

Brown took his foot off the hook and slithered on to the floor. He was exhausted. He stayed on his back a metre away from the door for a few minutes.

Angel busied himself tidying up the rope and the hook.

Brown raised himself up on one elbow and looked across at Angel.

Angel approached him. 'Are you all right?'

He didn't reply but quickly got to his feet.

He smiled.

Angel thought it was a smile. It was hard to be certain. It was very close to how he looked when he was in pain.

'I want to thank you most sincerely for saving my life,' Brown said, and he held out his hand to Angel. Angel took it. It was icy cold and had a grip of steel.

Brown gave one shake. Then the smile vanished. The face became motionless.

Tightening his grip, he straightened Angel's arm and, pressing his other big hand on Angel's elbow, whipped him round in a rapid circular motion towards the door, putting him centimetres from the edge. Angel grabbed hold of a handle on the wheel, kept hold of Brown and used the momentum to make another more powerful half circle to reverse their positions. Brown stumbled, reached out for something to hold on to, caught Angel's foot with both hands as he rolled out through the door and dropped out into the night.

Angel grabbed out for the secure stand of the hoist wheel as Brown pulled him by his foot halfway out of the door. He held on tight.

Brown screamed, 'Help me, Angel! Help me! Pull me up!'

Angel knew that he could not let go of the stand. He was thinking what he could do. 'Hold on, Brown! Hold on!'

'I can't hold on much longer,' Brown whined.

Angel could not loosen his grip on the wheel or else they *both* might be lost. Then he felt his shoe move. The heel had dropped.

Brown screamed. It was so piercing it made Angel catch his breath.

His shoe jerked off his foot entirely and the weight on his foot, leg and body was suddenly gone.

Brown was falling into the cold, black night sky.

Brown screamed again . . . a long scream that faded in the blackness.

Angel's stomach turned over and came up to his mouth as he visualised Brown hitting the hard tarmac.

Angel dragged himself into the building and slumped down on the floor, behind the wheel. He closed his eyes and quickly muttered, 'Oh my God. Forgive me for anything I have done to bring about his death . . . or anything I failed to do to avoid his death. Forgive me. Forgive me.'

Moments later, he stood up, and, hobbling without his left shoe, closed the doors and locked them. Then he dropped down to his position on the floor behind the wheel again, took out his mobile and phoned the station. Sergeant Clifton answered.

'Bernie, I want a pair of leather shoes size eight and half, the pathologist, and SOCO, ASAP.'

'It's two o'clock in the morning, sir. Are you sure you don't want anything else?'

'Yes, Bernie. I want a cup of tea.'

FIFTEEN

It was ten o'clock that same Wednesday morning, 30 November.

The body of Ezra Brown had been taken away in the mortuary van to the hospital for the pathologist to examine.

Angel's shoe had been photographed in situ on the mill car park, fifteen metres from the body of Ezra Brown, and taken into evidence.

Reg Smith had been released from the iron bed to which he had been handcuffed and was now in cell number four in Bromersley Police Station.

A fully loaded Smith & Wesson was found under the pillow of Smith's bed. He was charged with possession of that gun until the long list of offences he had committed had been determined by Angel in consultation the Crown Prosecution Service.

Angel handed in the old Walther to the armourer that he and Brown had fought over seconds before Brown fell out of the hoist door. He secretly held on to the Beretta and would bury it in the garden at the first opportunity.

He was very tired. He thought he would sleep for a fortnight. He drove home, garaged the car, and went to bed.

* * *

The following morning, Thursday, 1 December, Angel was back in his office, refreshed, washed, shaved, fed and ready to go.

Mary was returning tomorrow, and he was determined to have the murderer of the priest and the two nuns sewn up before he went to collect her. Also, he wanted to leave the office early that day to shop for some milk and bread, vacuum round the house, wash the pots and generally tidy up. And possibly buy some flowers. Mary loved flowers in the house.

But at that time, he had an appointment with Bishop Letterman, who had just arrived.

'Good to see you again, Inspector,' he said, removing his biretta and lowering his briefcase to the floor. 'Although I wish these were in happier circumstances.'

Angel shook his warm hand.

'Sit down, please, Bishop,' Angel said. 'And it gives me no joy to search for a serial murderer among people in holy orders, I assure you.'

The Bishop nodded. 'You were asking about Sister Clare? I looked up her file, which was not very informative. It simply said that her parents were practising Christians, attending church regularly, and that they brought her up in that tradition. After university she became a teacher and took a job in a school in London. After a few years, she said that she felt she had a vocation to serve God. That's all. I brought the file. Never been in trouble. You can read it for yourself.'

He put the biretta under his arm, opened the briefcase, took out a beige file and passed it to Angel.

The inspector read the relevant material and then looked at her conduct as reported by the Reverend Mother each year. It was a long column of 'Good' or 'Very good'. Clare had been a nun for more than twenty years. Angel passed the file back to the Bishop, who put it back in the briefcase, put the case down at his feet and removed the biretta from under his arm.

'So, where do you go from here, Inspector?'

'A good question,' Angel said. 'I shall have to rely on science.'

The Bishop blinked and then frowned.

'You see, I believe that there is evidence that the murderer must play a stringed musical instrument,' Angel added. 'Well, at the very least be very much among them, such as repairers or maybe players of other instruments, in an orchestra or a band.'

The Bishop's mouth dropped open.

'And I think you can help me,' Angel continued. 'On each of the victims was found, among other items, the finest grains of resin.'

'Resin?'

'I've heard that you're fond of music.'

The Bishop licked his lips. 'Yes, I am,' he said. Then he cleared his throat and added, 'I play the violin.'

There was a pause.

Angel said, 'Do you play regularly?'

'I try to practice every day, thirty minutes at least . . . depends on what else I have to do. My work as a priest has to be my priority. I try to play scales and exercises to keep my fingers nimble . . . and I may be learning a new piece for a concert.'

'How often do you have to use your resin block?'

'Not often. But I have used it more often recently because I had a broken string and had to replace it with a new one.'

Angel shook his head, gave a small sigh.

The Bishop's face whitened. His eyes flashed. 'You're not suggesting that I could be the murderer, Inspector?'

Without conviction, Angel said, 'No, of course not. But as you had a relationship of a sort with all three victims, I shall have to ask you where you were at the various times of the murders. I'll get my sergeant to go through the dates and times with you.'

Angel reached over for the phone.

The Bishop fidgeted with his biretta, running his hands centimetre by centimetre at a time round its rim.

* * *

'Good morning, Sister,' Angel said.

Sister Emma was sitting on her bed reading her missal as he entered her cell.

'Are we looking after you?' he said. 'Are you tolerably comfortable?'

She carefully placed a prayer card in the missal, closed it and put it on the bed at her side. 'I am all right here, Inspector. What can I do for you?'

Angel sat down on the other bed. 'Just a few questions to try to tidy things up.'

'I'm ready for the interrogation.'

Angel smiled. He wanted her to be at ease. 'It's not so much an interrogation as a chat.'

'All right, let's chat.'

Angel looked into her eyes. 'Are you considering revoking your confession at all?'

'No.'

'Why did you murder these three people, Emma? You must have had a motive — a stronger one than the one you've given me?'

'Inspector, that is something between my Saviour God and myself. And I will face whatever earthly punishment is coming to me.'

'If it was explained in court to the sentencing judge, the judge might ameliorate your sentence. You see, Sister, I haven't any actual evidence that you committed the murders. There is lots of circumstantial evidence, but no proof.'

'Surely you don't need proof if you have a voluntary confession?' Her eyes darted from place to place, avoiding eye contact with him.

'Tell me, Sister, do you play a musical instrument?'

She frowned and looked closely into his eyes. 'No.'

'Have you any South Asian heritage?'

She frowned again. 'No. Inspector, I don't know why you're doing all this prying and poking around, asking what seem like inconsequential questions . . . after all, at each murder, I was there. I had the opportunity. I had the weapon. I confessed I killed the three of them. I would have thought that you wouldn't need witnesses, or any conventional evidence. I've admitted that I'm guilty. Why all this time-wasting? Why don't you get on with it? Tell them to send me to prison for twenty years or whatever.'

* * *

Angel came away from Sister Emma disappointed that he had in no way changed her mind about anything, nor had he really found out anything new . . . except that she seemed more determined than ever to plead guilty.

He asked the duty jailer to admit him into Sister Clare's cell.

When Clare heard the keys tinkle she came up to the door to meet him.

Angel noticed her face was ashen.

'Is Sister Precious all right, Inspector? She'll be all by herself. And is it possible that she could visit me?'

'I saw her the day before yesterday and she was absolutely all right.'

Clare smiled and relaxed. He thought she must love the old nun a great deal.

'She can't still be on your suspects list or she would be in a cell like Emma and me, wouldn't she?' she said.

Angel raised his shoulders in a little shrug. 'Maybe. Maybe. I've come to ask you a few questions, Clare.'

'Oh?'

'Are you still in the same mind as before? Are you sticking by the confession you made?'

'Of course.'

Clare's eye was suddenly taken by the slide covering the food slot in the cell door. It moved open slightly.

Somebody was listening.

Angel had his back to the door and couldn't see anything of this.

'I don't understand,' he said. 'You must have had a motive for committing the three murders?'

169

Sister Clare didn't reply.

Angel's facial muscles tightened. 'If you don't tell me, I certainly can't help you.'

'I don't need your help, Inspector,' she said, fingering the silver crucifix on a cord around her neck. 'My help, if it is required — if you will excuse me saying so — will come from a much higher authority.'

Angel nodded. He accepted the answer.

Clare noticed the slide in the door of the cell close. The listener apparently had gone. She breathed out her relief. Then she said, 'Inspector, I asked if it was possible for Sister Precious to visit me?'

Angel frowned. 'Not unless it will progress the investigation and lead to proving the identity of the murderer of the priest and two of your sisters. And an officer such as myself would need to be present.'

Clare sighed. Her shoulders slumped and she put on a disappointed face. 'I can't see what difference it would make. You have my confession.'

Angel said, 'You're in a very serious position, Clare. You realise that if you stand by that confession, you could be imprisoned in the north of Scotland or some lonely place in the West Country where you might simply moulder away.'

'I hear you, Inspector,' she said. 'But wherever I am sent, the Lord will be there to greet me and watch over me.'

'Your sentence could be over thirty years. I hope your faith lasts the full term of your sentence.'

She breathed in deeply and then out. 'It will, Inspector. It certainly will. My natural life may not.'

* * *

Angel returned to the office with his bowed head and the disappointment etched on his face.

Carter rushed in. 'The Bishop isn't married. He lives alone, and he claims that he was in bed while the murders were being committed.'

Angel's face brightened. 'That's our man. He has keys to the convent. And he's the source of the resin. He has a lot to explain. Where is he now?'

'He wanted to speak to the two nuns in custody. I told him that he would have to see you. He asked if he could wait in your office until you returned. I thought that was all right, so I brought him here.'

Angel whipped round. 'Well, he isn't here now! Find him, and find him quickly. You make your way through the offices to reception and I'll work my way towards the cells and the rear entrance.'

Carter raced off.

Angel called into the detectives' office, saw DC Scrivens and enrolled him to search for the Bishop. Then he went to the cells and saw the duty jailer.

'Have you seen a Bishop, lad?'

'Yes, sir. I caught him hanging around here about ten minutes ago, when you were in with one of the nuns. He asked me how he could get out to the car park. I let him out through the rear door.'

'Ten minutes ago?'

'About that, sir. Yes.'

Angel flashed his plastic security card at the door lock and let himself out to the car park.

He looked around at the fifteen or twenty cars parked there. The Bishop was nowhere to be seen. He ran round the side of the station to the front and saw Scrivens coming out of the main door.

'Any luck?' Angel said.

Scrivens shook his head.

Angel sighed. He went back to the rear entrance, let himself in and asked the jailer to open Sister Emma's cell again.

She stood up looking alarmed as he came in. 'What's the matter?'

'I want to contact Bishop Letterman. Do you know where he lives?'

'Not exactly, Inspector,' she said. 'I know he oversees Michael and All Angels in Lower Foxted.'

'Never heard of it. Must be a little place. Have you got his home address?'

'No, but Sister Precious will have, and I know it's in the convent address book.'

'Thank you, Sister,' he said. Then he rushed out of the cell, took out his mobile and tapped in the convent's number.

Sister Precious soon rattled off the address and the mobile number. He wrote them in his book.

Angel tapped in the number. It rang for a long time but there was no reply. He had to get hold of Bishop Letterman urgently before he disappeared into the underworld.

He found DS Carter in the detective's office.

'Flora, I want you to come with me,' he said. 'We've got to get hold of the Bishop.'

They rushed off in Angel's car to Lower Foxted. He found out from the satnav that it was north-east of Bromersley in the middle of nowhere.

On the journey, he brought Carter up to date with developments and his thoughts.

About an hour later, a sign at the side of the road indicated that they had arrived in Lower Foxted. It was a village of thirty or forty houses, a big church, two pubs and a post office that sold everything from a pin to an elephant.

It was very quiet — the streets were empty, there were no pavements, and not much traffic.

Angel drove towards the church and saw a man in a khaki shirt, waistcoat and dungarees at the entrance to a barn adjacent to the street. He was looking up the road.

Carter asked him where Bishop Letterman lived.

'Listen out for a bow scraping on a string and you're there,' he said without a smile. Then he pointed to a cottage on the opposite side of the street. 'It's there.'

When Angel switched off the engine and opened the car door he could hear the sweet sounds of a violin playing 'Sheep May Safely Graze'.

Angel and Carter exchanged glances, got out of the car and made their way up to the front door. He pressed the bell. The music stopped and a few moments later the Bishop opened the door.

'Oh,' the Bishop said with a smile. 'This is a surprise . . . come on in, Inspector Angel, Sergeant Carter.'

They settled in a little room with a piano occupying most of the space, on top of which sat a violin and a pile of sheet music. The Bishop said, 'I suppose you've come to arrest me? This is all very upsetting. I'm a Bishop of the Anglican Church, for goodness sake. My job is to save lives . . . to comfort anybody in trouble . . . to support the two sisters accused of murder. I feel very bad about that. I just don't know how to help them. I've been praying and praying for guidance . . .'

Angel said, 'Bishop, if you can provide one convincing witness to where you were at the time of any of the murders, you will not be arrested. If you can give me a credible alternative explanation as to why resin was found on all three victims, you will not be arrested.'

'I must say, Inspector, I'm not the only person in the world to use resin.'

'Bishop, you're the only person in this community who has had recent contact with each of the victims and who plays a stringed musical instrument.'

'Why limit its use to stringed instruments?' the Bishop said. 'What about people who use glue?'

Angel's face dropped. 'Glue?' he said, as if he had just discovered the word.

'Yes. Model makers. Furniture makers. I should think most households in the country have a tube of glue somewhere on hand. Didn't you say there were also some traces of beeswax found on the bodies?'

'Yes,' Angel said dreamily. His eyes were darting everywhere, settling on things but not seeing them.

Carter said, 'That would be from the candles.'

'Yes, but resin and beeswax are both constituents of glue,' the Bishop said. 'I took chemistry at Cambridge before theology.'

Angel moved his head through several positions, not looking at anything. His eyes were half closed in thought. Then he suddenly stood up.

'Sorry to have disturbed you, Bishop. Please go back to the sheep. May they continue to safely graze. Come on, Flora. We've a lot to do.'

* * *

An hour later they were back at Bromersley Police Station. They went in through the rear entrance and Angel asked the duty jailer to open up Sister Clare's cell.

Clare looked worried as Angel and Carter came in.

'What now?' she said.

Angel said, 'Sister Clare, we now have sufficient proof of the actual murderer and it isn't you. You are discharged immediately. Nevertheless, we are considering bringing charges against you for wasting police time. I presume you'll want to return to the convent.'

Clare at first smiled and then her expression changed. She looked concerned. 'I'm sure that Sister Precious didn't do it, Inspector,' she said. 'She's too old, too small and she simply couldn't commit such serious crimes. Her faith is too strong.'

'I know, and I'll take your comments into consideration, Sister,' Angel said. 'I'll have a car waiting for you at the front of the station in five minutes.'

Angel then looked at Carter. 'Come on, Flora.'

They made for the door, and Clare said, 'But, Inspector—'

The door closed.

Angel turned to the duty jailer. 'Constable, will you let us into Sister Emma's cell?'

As they waited in the corridor while the constable found the key to open the cell, Carter was quiet and thoughtful. 'You're not really going to prefer charges against her for wasting police time, are you?'

174

'Probably not, but it's as well to give her something to worry about. Besides,' he said with a grin, 'if everybody pleaded guilty to every crime that popped up we'd be out of work.'

Emma was seated on her bed, reading her missal. She looked up as Angel and Carter came in.

'Come in, come in,' she said, trying to be light-hearted. 'It's not often I have visitors. Sit down. I'm afraid I can only offer you this other bed.'

Angel said, 'Sister Emma, I have to tell you that I'm accepting your confession of murdering the priest and two of your sisters. In a moment, DS Carter will be formally charging you.'

Emma's mouth opened but she said nothing.

'Do you want your confession to stand?'

She couldn't speak, just wiped her mouth with a tissue. She breathed in and out deeply, and her bottom lip trembled.

'Yes,' she said quietly.

Angel went on. 'From your application to join the order, you said that your mother was a nun here years ago. Sister Vera. She had a relationship with a man — a priest — and became pregnant. When she confessed to the Reverend Mother, she was discharged.'

Emma found her tongue.

Her red eyes stood out. 'She was a bitch. A woman pretending to be a goodie-goodie when all the time she was evil . . . She revelled in her role as Reverend Mother — pretending to be all sweetness and light, bowing and scraping to all and sundry. If the truth be known, she was a monster.'

'What happened to your father?'

'He disappeared into the night,' Emma said. 'All I knew about him was that he was a priest. Mummy never mentioned his name. She died when I was thirteen. That was hard to take.'

'What happened to you then?'

'I went to live with Granny, my mother's mother, but she wasn't well and died three years later. That was awful again. *Another* funeral. I wasn't ready for all these disasters.'

Angel nodded.

'However, I could begin to see what I had to do. To put things right. To make things fair. It was not *only* my mother's fault that I was born, even though what she did was wrong. Excusable, but wrong. It takes two to make a baby. But I had absolutely nothing to go on about the priest, my father. So I vowed to repay the horrid Reverend Mother and the nuns that were here at that time. I would close this order down and everybody that had anything to do with it. So, after a dreadful time as a teenager, getting lots of jobs in offices, factories and shops, resulting in a lot of unwelcome attention from my typically male bosses, when I was eighteen I applied to be a nun in this order.'

Then she stopped and looked at Angel. 'But how are you able to prove it was me who committed the murders?'

'Science came to our aid. It all came together today when somebody mentioned *glue*. The tiny particles of dust sampled from the clothes of the three victims revealed quantities of their own skin, resin, charcoal and beeswax . . . and in two instances, two human hairs that DNA profiling said came from South Asia. I knew that some Indian girls and women grew their hair to sell to make wigs or hair pieces, which often have to be glued in position. And I found out that the glue for that was made from resin and beeswax. I understand you have hair loss problems — for me, your involvement was proven.'

Emma suddenly stood up, grabbed the pillow off the bed and threw it across the cell. 'You don't understand. Nobody understands. Life isn't worth living if you have alopecia.'

Undeterred, Angel continued. 'I took it for granted that when you went on holiday, you would break another rule of the order, to stay in your very best habit and keep yourself smart and clean throughout your leave. I expect you dumped the habit and wimple and put on your glad rags, fixed your hair, made up your face and went out on the town.'

Emma's face suddenly turned sour. She jumped up, arms in the air.

'You're too bloody clever for your own good,' she screamed, spittle flying everywhere. 'Get out. Get out! *Get out!*'

Angel stood up and turned to Carter. 'Get on with it, Flora.'

Carter stood up. She looked at the tall, red-faced young woman and began, 'Sister Emma of the Convent of the Holy Reliquary of the Finger of Saint Ethel, you are being charged with the murders of—'

'Yes, and I am guilty, and I would do it all over again!' Emma shrieked.

* * *

It was Friday, 2 December, and the alarm on the clock at the side of Angel's bed rang loud and clear to tell him it was 7.15 a.m.

He woke up with a smile on his face. It was the day he was to meet Mary's train at Bromersley station at 4.45 p.m., and he was adamant that nothing would hinder his welcoming home of the wonderful, beautiful Mary.

It had been a tough week without her and he was looking forward to more of the married bliss he had enjoyed with her over the years. Also, he had avoided having to spend any of his leave in Edinburgh with the irritable, irresponsible, man-mad butterfly personality of Miriam, Mary's divorced sister.

He arrived at his office at 8.30 a.m. and was wading through the pile of correspondence that had accumulated when his mobile phone rang. It was Sister Precious.

'Inspector Angel?' she said. 'The Lord has looked kindly down upon us and answered our prayers.'

Angel smiled. 'Why? What's happened, Sister?'

'I have the most wonderful news. Cheapo's, the big national supermarket, has taken a ten-year lease of Duxbury Mill.'

His eyes danced with delight as she spoke.

'That's great news, Sister.'

'I've been into the chapel, given thanks and lit a special candle. They were suddenly in need of several thousand cubic metres of storage space in or near Bromersley. They intend to install a goods lift and a security system this weekend, and they need the key. Now, I'm going out shopping this morning. May I call at the station and pick it up from you in a few minutes? It is required most urgently.'

'That's good news, Sister. Of course, I'll leave the key in reception. The regular additional income will make your community's living conditions much better, won't it?'

'Oh no. Our standard of living will remain the same, Inspector. The extra income will go to our charities, who are all in desperate straits.'

Angel wrinkled his brow.

* * *

Angel was beginning to feel excited when the 4.45 diesel train thundered into Bromersley train station and squeaked its way to a gentle stop.

Doors banged open. Faces and cases appeared. Hissing noise came from the engine.

Angel scanned the doors and windows along the platform for Mary. He was aching to see her. His heart yearned for her. It was a passion which, after all these years, he found difficult to explain and impossible to control.

And then he saw her . . . framed in the doorway, looking round for him. Their eyes met.

The pangs in his chest gently ached. His eyes watered.

He hadn't realised till now just how much he loved her.

He smiled, took off his hat and waved it. She saw him and smiled. It was a wonderful smile.

If Cecil B. DeMille had been making a picture, he would have demanded an immediate close-up.

Angel made his way to the carriage door through the stream of passengers making their way to the exit gate in the opposite direction.

He reached her. She was now standing on the platform next to her suitcase.

'Darling!' he said.

They kissed. Angel thought she held herself back from him a little.

'Oh, sweetheart,' he said, 'it's great to have you home. I *have* missed you.'

'Darling,' she said. 'Would you help Miriam with her case?'

'Hello, Michael,' said a familiar female voice.

Angel looked across and saw Miriam climbing down the carriage steps, immaculately dressed as if for Ascot, with an angelic smile on her face that had caused a stirring in many a man's loins.

Angel changed. He sighed, shook his head, then looked at Mary, who tried to look apologetic.

With gritted teeth, he reached out to the open carriage door for Miriam's heavy suitcase.

THE END

ALSO BY ROGER SILVERWOOD

YORKSHIRE MURDER MYSTERIES
Book 1: THE MISSING NURSE
Book 2: THE MISSING WIFE
Book 3: THE MAN IN THE PINK SUIT
Book 4: THE MORALS OF A MURDERER
Book 5: THE AUCTION MURDERS
Book 6: THE MISSING KILLER
Book 7: THE UMBRELLA MURDERS
Book 8: THE MISSING MILLIONAIRE
Book 9: THE MISSING THIEF
Book 10: FIND THE LADY
Book 11: THE MISSING MODEL
Book 12: MURDER IN BARE FEET
Book 13: THE MISSING HUSBAND
Book 14: THE CUCKOO CLOCK MURDERS
Book 15: SHRINE TO MURDER
Book 16: THE SNUFFBOX MURDERS
Book 17: THE DOG COLLAR MURDERS
Book 18: THE CHESHIRE CAT MURDERS
Book 19: THE DIAMOND ROSARY MURDERS
Book 20: THIRTEEN STEPS TO MURDER
Book 21: THE FRUIT GUM MURDERS
Book 22: THE MONEY TREE MURDERS
Book 23: ANGEL AND THE ACTRESS
Book 24: THE MURDER LIST
Book 25: THE LIPSTICK MURDERS
Book 26: THE MUSIC BOX MURDERS
Book 27: MURDER ON TIME
Book 28: ANGEL'S FINAL PROBLEM?
Book 29: ANGEL AND THE NUN

STANDALONE
THE GUILTY DAUGHTER

Thank you for reading this book.

If you enjoyed it please leave feedback on Amazon or Goodreads, and if there is anything we missed or you have a question about, then please get in touch. We appreciate you choosing our book.

Founded in 2014 in Shoreditch, London, we at Joffe Books pride ourselves on our history of innovative publishing. We were thrilled to be shortlisted for Independent Publisher of the Year at the British Book Awards.

www.joffebooks.com

We're very grateful to eagle-eyed readers who take the time to contact us. Please send any errors you find to corrections@joffebooks.com. We'll get them fixed ASAP.